Wild Heart's Haven

WAGON TRAIN MATCHES

LACY WILLIAMS

Prologue

ONLY MINUTES after the wagon train travelers celebrated his brother August's wedding, Owen Mason approached the creek, picking his way through the woods so he wouldn't disturb the woman he was seeking. The place in his shoulder where he'd been winged by a bullet pulsed with a dull, never-ending ache.

Rachel Duncan knelt on the bank of the little tributary, her hands submerged in the water, suds trailing downstream. As she scrubbed her hands together, he realized she was washing out her dress.

She owned exactly two dresses. One she wore now, that his new sister-in-law, Felicity, had modified to fit her in this late stage of her pregnancy. And the one she was washing, the dress she'd been wearing when she'd been found in the woods over a week ago.

He didn't want to know so much about her. How many dresses she owned. That she was restless at night, didn't sleep much thanks to the baby she carried. How she looked when she grieved.

No one else seemed to be aware that she was down here while the rest of camp was packed up, folks standing around congratulating August and Felicity on their nuptials. It was only a matter of time before Hollis would blow the bugle.

But Rachel seemed to be in no hurry.

He stood several yards downstream and half-hidden behind a tree. She'd been nothing but trouble since his brother had found her out in the woods.

Trouble for Owen.

Who couldn't stop thinking about her. Especially after he'd watched her brother's life leak out between his hands.

He hadn't put Daniel on that wagon or forced him to take off from the main caravan. Owen had been shouting for the other man to stop and take cover when the outlaws had started shooting. Owen had shot back, wanting to scare them off.

In the melee, he couldn't be sure whose bullet had hit Daniel, his or one of the outlaws'.

It didn't matter. Daniel was gone. Maybe that was for the better. The man had been cruel, drowned his grief in a bottle, said things to his sister that no man should ever say to a woman. Struck her, even.

As far as Owen was concerned, good riddance.

But once Owen had delivered Daniel's body into the circle of wagons, Rachel had shut down.

Gone was the woman who had harangued every family on the wagon train, trying to find a horse or some other transportation to take her back East.

Gone was the woman who'd helped every woman who would let her—toting wash water, making supper, watching children.

It was as if Rachel had died that day too, and only her

shadow remained. She was meek and quiet, barely ate. He noticed her staring blankly into a fire when he woke and last thing before bed.

He wasn't supposed to feel guilt over her situation.

But he did.

And it made him itchy.

And that made him mad.

He made his way up the creek bank, now making no effort to hide or quiet his approach.

She didn't look up.

His temper rumbled like a sleeping dragon, a wisp of smoke on an exhale. Why couldn't the woman do anything the way he might expect?

He cleared his throat.

When she still didn't look up, he asked, "You doin' all right?"

She didn't answer him, just kept scrubbing that dress under the water. He'd been close enough to see the fraying hems and an elbow that had already been patched. If she wasn't careful, she'd scrub the thing to threads.

Silence reigned for a moment that lengthened into awkwardness and the dragon that was his temper flared its nostrils, a lick of flame escaping. "I asked you a question."

She looked up at him, only dullness in her eyes. "I'm fine. Is that what you want to hear?"

If her words had held any of the old fire she'd always flamed at him, he would've kept his trap shut. But she spoke almost in monotone.

"Is the baby all right? After that fall?" He'd been too far away, on horseback, to do anything when her scoundrel of a brother had shoved her off the wagon. He'd seen it, though, and something inside of him had raged when she'd hit the ground with a limp thud.

She shrugged. Her indifference poked the dragon.

"I'm trying to help," he snapped. "The least you could do is answer me."

Something inside her seemed to snap, too. She threw down the dress, splashing droplets everywhere. "The least I can do?" She struggled to her feet, her eyes now flashing fire. "I don't want your help. Your help got my brother killed."

Her words hit him like a slug to the stomach, stealing his air. It didn't matter that her brother had been a scoundrel. Owen had been responsible.

"You're still stuck with me until we reach the fort." This time, his words held only a little of the bite from earlier.

Tears sprang to her eyes before she turned her head and stomped after the dress that had quickly floated downstream —in his direction.

He took two steps into the water and caught it, his wound pulsing with the effort. He held the sopping mass of cloth over the creek as water ran down in rivulets.

She didn't want to be left at the fort. That much was obvious. He didn't blame her. The fort would be filled with crass men, and who knew how long it might be before someone was willing to take her on—maybe an eternity if she still intended to go back East.

She firmed her lips and her chin tipped up. His stomach dipped at the show of attitude. She might be grieving, but she was still herself. That fiery attitude hiding under the layers of pain.

She reached for the dress.

He took the time to squeeze most of the water out of it before he handed it to her.

4

She didn't say thank you.

He shook his head. What had he expected? "Hollis will call for us to move out in a few minutes."

He was done here. He'd said what he needed to say.

"If you really wanted to help, you'd find me a way back East," she muttered to the ground.

He stopped from where he'd moved a step away. Put his hands on his hips as he faced her again.

"Everyone here is traveling West," he reminded her as gently as he could.

Maybe not so gentle, judging by the stubborn twist of her lips.

"What you need is a husband." The words leapt out before he realized he was going to say them.

Fire flashed in her eyes. "You offering?"

No. The answer rang inside him like a bell, clear and loud. He wasn't husband material, and she sure as shootin' wasn't a match for him.

But a part of him niggled like a tooth waiting to fall out. He had been responsible, at least in part, for Daniel's death.

Did that make him responsible for her?

"I guess I am."

She looked as surprised as he felt that he'd said the words.

But she didn't give him a chance to change his mind. "Fine."

Fine.

Only it wasn't fine at all.

What had he done?

One

"HOLLIS WILL BE out with the lead wagon."

The woman walking beside Owen Mason barely acknowledged his words, and he felt a stirring of irritation. He worked to quash it.

Rachel Duncan might be the stubbornest, most independent woman he'd ever met. Her dark honey-colored hair and blue-eyed gaze might've been pleasing if not for the irritation he felt every time she opened her mouth to speak. She bothered him like a burr under his saddle. Made his skin itch like it was crawling with ants.

And Owen had promised to marry her.

That's why he needed Hollis Tremblay, the wagon master of their company. To perform the ceremony.

The sun had been up for almost an hour. The wagon train camp along the Platte River was bustling with activity as every traveler, even the children, helped prepare to pull out for the day. Their caravan had been on the trail West to Oregon for weeks now, and the company knew the routine for readying for a day of travel.

7

Owen needed to find Hollis, fast. The bugle—the signal to pull out—was about to blow. He skirted a girl no older than ten who was trying to shoo two chickens into a large wicker basket.

"Sorry."

He glanced over his shoulder at Rachel's murmured apology to see chickens scattering in opposite directions. The girl's basket was on the ground, and she was glaring at Rachel.

Rachel had one hand pressed against her opposite elbow, as if she'd bumped it.

Probably bumped it on the little girl. Had she run into her?

It was plausible, given Rachel's condition. The woman was due to give birth in the next few weeks. He doubted she could see her feet when she was standing up, and she was clumsy. He'd seen it himself, watched her knock over a pail of fresh water from the creek because she hadn't seen it on the ground in front of her.

She caught his gaze and her lips pinched. She always wore a sour expression when she looked at him.

Guilt surged. Maybe he deserved it.

The wound in his arm—a thin line between a scrape and a cut on the outside of his biceps—pulsed in time with his heartbeat. He slowed his stride slightly so she could keep up, but the urgency inside him didn't go away.

He wanted to get this over with.

Owen came across Leo Spencer and his wife, near their wagon. His older half-brother had fallen in love on the earliest days of the trail and married Evangeline.

Their campsite was packed up. The fire had been stamped out. Evangeline's young sister, Sara, played on the wagon seat, away from the dangerous hooves of the oxen already in their traces.

Judging by the way he and Evangeline stood so close against the wagon, Leo must've thought everyone else around was too busy to pay attention. Leo was the same height as Owen, and sometimes looking at him was akin to looking at Owen's own reflection. They both resembled their late father with his dark hair and eyes.

Leo had his arms around Evangeline's waist, and as Owen watched, he raised one hand to brush against Evangeline's cheek. The clear affection and love in Leo's expression twisted Owen up inside.

It didn't matter. Owen had no use for a love match. Or any match at all. He was only going through with this because it was the right thing to do.

Leo must've caught sight of Owen striding through camp because he glanced over his shoulder and then dropped his hand, though he didn't look embarrassed to be caught snuggling his wife.

"You seen Hollis?" Owen called.

Leo shook his head negatively. "You seen Coop?"

"I haven't," Owen responded. Coop was Leo's younger brother, no relation to Owen.

Owen halted abruptly and Rachel almost plowed into him. He stopped her forward momentum with a hand on her elbow, though he quickly dropped it, shaking out the ache from his wound.

She gave him a squinty-eyed glare when he turned to her. "Why don't you wait here? I'll go fetch Hollis."

"It will be quicker if I go with you."

He couldn't recall a conversation with Rachel where she hadn't argued with him. Irritation stung like nettles all over his skin. He rolled his shoulders to try and get rid of the feeling. The pulse of pain in his arm grew more intense and then faded.

"We'll need witnesses anyway." He was aware of Leo's sharp sideways glance, but continued, "Just stay put."

He heard the gurgle of her stomach. His eyebrows raised of their own volition. "Have you eaten anything today?"

Her frown was answer enough.

He looked past Rachel to Evangeline, who was speaking to Sara. He called out, "Can you help Rachel scrounge up some breakfast?"

Evangeline murmured a quiet, "Of course," but he was already striding away, intent on finding Hollis so he could get this over with.

Leo jogged to fall into step beside Owen.

"What do you need Hollis for? And witnesses?"

Owen wasn't used to being on the other end of Leo's big brother inquisition. Leo was three years older, which made Owen the same age as Collin and Coop, Leo's twin brothers from another father.

Owen had grown up in California, never knowing he had a brother and sister until his father had been dying of consumption and revealed it on his deathbed. Owen had made a difficult decision to go back east to try and find his siblings.

He was used to being the older brother. The problem solver. The responsible one.

And Owen had found them in a spot of trouble.

Leo hadn't wanted anything to do with Owen those first weeks. Owen thought things had smoothed over between them, but that muscle ticking in his brother's jaw maybe meant things were still a little tumultuous.

"What do you need Hollis for?" Leo repeated.

Owen might as well tell him. It wasn't easy to keep secrets on the trail. With only a flimsy piece of canvas between you and your next neighbor, it was far too easy to overhear conversations.

"I'm marrying Rachel."

Leo snorted, but then grew serious when he realized Owen wasn't joking. "You can't marry her. You hate each other."

"I don't hate her." He couldn't say she felt the same. Not for certain.

At their first meeting, she had been pointing a gun—empty at the time, but he hadn't known that—at Owen's younger brother, August. So Owen had tackled her to the ground. She'd been terrified, hiding from the men who had massacred her wagon train, and it had been dark. He hadn't realized until everything was over that she was a *she*, and that she was pregnant.

Even if she had forgiven him for that, there was other bad blood between them.

"Maybe you don't hate her, but you sure don't like her."

Leo was right. Owen and Rachel couldn't seem to help arguing at every turn.

He sighed and stopped, turning to face his brother.

"It's my fault Daniel got himself killed." It was the first time he'd said the words out loud. But not the first time he'd thought them.

Leo's frown deepened. "How d'you figure? Daniel was a bully who tried to steal a horse, then tried to steal a wagon."

Rachel's brother had been shot in the middle of a gunfight when Owen and Leo and the others from their company had been defending against an outlaw band who'd

tried to murder them and steal their supplies and animals—
the same outlaw band that had killed Rachel's other family.

"I should've tied him hand and foot," Owen said.

Or had one of the younger men hold him at gunpoint.
Maybe given him a horse and sent him on his way.

Any choice but the one Owen had made could've resulted
in a different outcome.

The other men from the wagon train—including the one
Daniel had attempted to steal a horse from—had wanted him
hanged. Owen had thought he was sparing Daniel's life to
bring him to the fort.

Daniel hadn't survived that long.

And Owen might never forget the keening wail Rachel
had let out when she'd seen her brother's lifeless body.

Leo's voice shook him out of that terrible memory. "Guilt
isn't something to build a marriage on."

Leo was as serious as Owen had ever seen him. His voice
held an edge Owen hadn't heard in weeks.

But at Leo's words, Owen felt his shoulders relax. "It's
only until we reach Oregon," he told his brother. "Then we'll
have it annulled."

Leo scowled.

"What?" Owen was honestly confused at his brother's
response.

"You'd marry her and walk away?" Now Leo sounded
offended. And as far as Owen was concerned, this wasn't his
business.

"This isn't a love match." Owen couldn't help it. He bristled at Leo's commanding tone. "It's an agreement between
the two of us."

Leo sneered. "It sounds like something our pa would've
done. He left one wife behind easily enough."

Was that what Leo was worried about? "I won't leave her penniless."

Leo shook his head. "I thought you were different. But there's a lot of Pa in you, isn't there?"

Owen took offense to that. "Our father was an upstanding man. A man of honor—"

"Except when he walked away from his family."

Leo's words felt like a slap. He wasn't done yet. "And you're gonna do the same. There's nothing honorable in what you're doing."

Leo whirled on his heel and stomped off, leaving Owen fuming. He strode through a couple of parked wagons, grateful there weren't any travelers nearby to have heard the words exchanged by the brothers.

Leo had no right to talk to him that way. Leo didn't understand.

Owen was trying to do right by Rachel. Maybe it wasn't entirely his fault that her brother was a no-account thief who didn't mind bullying his pregnant sister when he got drunk. But he'd been a part of what had happened.

Marrying Rachel meant she'd have the protection of his name until they reached Oregon. That was enough to settle the debt between them.

It didn't matter whether Leo liked it or not. Owen had lived his entire life, until the past nine months, believing he was the older brother. He'd been raised to do the right thing. Take responsibility. He took care of his own. He was a man.

And he was man enough to make this decision.

* * *

Rachel felt blood boiling in her face as she stood at Owen's side in front of Hollis.

The wagon master's brown-skinned face held a solemn expression. He was clean shaven and his dark brown eyes assessed her coolly from beneath his hat.

Prickles of awareness skittered over her skin, as if too many eyes were watching her. Owen had chosen a spot out of the way of foot traffic, blocked from the view of most of the company by a couple of parked wagons. So maybe the itch between her shoulder blades was her imagination. Or a result of her misgivings.

Owen's brother August was the only person she considered a friend on the wagon train. He stood slightly behind the two of them with his slender, beautiful wife Felicity at his side. The two witnesses she and Owen needed for their marriage to be valid.

It was telling that Leo Spencer hadn't reappeared when Owen had returned with Hollis.

She'd seen the way Leo had looked at her when he'd trotted off with Owen. She recognized the way he'd spoken to his brother. Arguing, that's what he'd done.

He didn't approve of her.

It seemed no one in this company did.

Hollis and Owen exchanged a wordless glance and her stomach dipped for a moment.

"You find me one person who will speak up for him," the wagon master had pointed to Daniel. *"One person, and we'll take the two of you to the fort like my captains promised."*

She blinked away the memory of the hard light in the wagon master's eyes, but the echo of that threat still burned like icy fire in her bones. Owen was one of the captains. Marrying him meant she would be a captain's wife. She couldn't be abandoned out here in the wild if she was a captain's wife.

Hollis moved his intense stare to Rachel. "You sure this is what you want?"

She couldn't forget her precarious position on the wagon train. Her voice caught as she replied, "I'm certain."

Owen didn't so much as twitch beside her. She couldn't help an awareness of the man anytime he was near. He was several inches taller than Evan had been. Her Evan had preferred a clean shave, while Owen sported several days' worth of dark stubble, as if he was too busy for neat grooming. Not unkempt. Just scruffy.

Hollis didn't ask them to face each other, just started reading from the prayer book he held in his hands.

"We're gathered here in the sight of God and these witnesses..."

She couldn't help thinking how different this was from her wedding to Evan, only two years ago.

The morning sun was beating down on her head and a breeze tugged strands of her hair into her eyes. The camp was noisy, with oxen bawling and children shouting. A dog barked.

When she'd married Evan, there'd been a reverent hush in the small church that she'd attended faithfully with her parents since she'd been a small girl. Her father had given her away. Her mother had sniffled back tears from the first pew.

Evan had faced her, his hands trembling slightly when he clasped hers.

Owen didn't so much as look at her.

"...considering the causes for which matrimony was ordained. First, for the procreation of children..."

She ignored the sudden smarting of tears behind her nose.

Evan would never know his child, the one she'd carried for eight months. He'd died violently, suddenly, a mere two weeks ago.

"...a remedy against sin and to avoid fornication..."

Hollis's words barely registered as she stared straight ahead. And when they did, she couldn't help the sniff. Owen could barely stand her. Surely she was the last person he'd want in that way.

They both knew this marriage was in name only. He'd said as much when he'd proposed to her—such as it was. He didn't think of her like that, and she had no romantic inclinations toward him. This was an agreement, only in place until they reached Oregon.

"...for the mutual society, help, and comfort that the one ought to have for the other, both in prosperity and adversity."

Now Owen did twitch. His head tipped slightly toward her. She'd registered the movement before she'd thought better of it and found herself caught in his blue-eyed gaze. He would've been handsome, if she could stand him.

She should feel a pang of guilt, shouldn't she? Hollis's words as part of the ceremony—such as it was—were the crux of her dilemma. She needed Owen's company, needed his help.

His eyes narrowed slightly and she dropped her gaze.

She couldn't imagine the man offering her comfort. Not with the way he felt about her. The way they felt about each other.

His name and his help were enough.

She still couldn't understand why he'd made the offer to marry her, but she wasn't fool enough to turn it down.

She had nothing to offer him. No worldly goods. No money. He couldn't want her company.

But it mattered not what his motives were. He'd promised to get her to Oregon. Somehow, she'd beg or borrow money to tag along with an eastbound company. Go home.

More tears smarted at the thought of the small cottage she'd shared with Evan—sold now, and most of their furniture with it. Of her mother, back in the small town where Rachel had grown up. Rachel blinked the tears away.

The baby twisted strongly inside her and she couldn't hold back a small gasp. She pressed one hand against the lower part of her belly. This earned a look from both Owen and Hollis.

"Keep going?" Hollis asked.

Face flushed, she nodded.

"If any man can show just cause why these two should not be married, let him speak now or forever hold his peace."

For a moment, her chest locked tight with a breath that wouldn't draw. Would August speak?

I can't marry you. Not when my heart belongs to someone else. In a fit of desperation, she'd asked August to marry her, to protect her. He'd chosen Felicity instead. The two of them were clearly in love. He had to know Rachel was marrying his brother for mercenary reasons.

Surely August had concerns. Maybe the same ones Leo had.

But no one spoke until Hollis cleared his throat. "You two gonna face each other?"

It seemed to take an interminably long time for Owen's feet to shift. She hadn't intended to move until he did. When they fully faced each other, there was a faint frown on his lips.

"Clasp hands," Hollis said.

"That's all right—"

"No, thank you—"

Owen's refusal, spoken at the same time as Rachel's prim words, made August cough. Or was he covering a laugh? She found herself frowning. What made Owen balk over holding hands with her?

Hollis wasn't amused. "That wasn't a question. You want me to continue or not?"

There was a long beat before Owen reached out both hands, palms up.

Warily, she slipped her hands into his larger ones. His clasp was warm and dry.

"Wilt thou have this woman as thy wedded wife... Wilt thou love her, comfort her, honor and keep her... as long as ye both shall live?"

Hollis's words knocked into her with the same force she'd felt that first night when Owen had tackled her to the ground.

It isn't real. But it didn't matter what she told herself.

There was no ignoring that the vows he'd asked Owen to agree to were the same ones that Evan had spoken two years ago. She felt as if she couldn't breathe.

"Owen," Hollis prompted.

His hesitation had grown noticeably long.

There was a fine line between his brows as he stared into her face. "I will."

Relief flowed over her, until Hollis said, "Wilt thou have this man to be thy husband..."

It isn't real. It's not a true marriage.

But no matter how much she argued with herself, the panicky feeling twisting inside her was a reminder that she was speaking these vows before God.

I can't do this.

"...obey him, and serve him, love, honor, and..."

She must do it. Say the words. Bind herself to Owen.

"I will," she whispered when Hollis finished speaking.

Owen was completely impassive. No hint of emotion crossed his expression. This was what she'd bound herself to for the duration of this journey?

It didn't matter. Couldn't. She didn't need him to care about her, to like her as a friend. She only needed to ensure her place on the wagon train.

But Hollis wasn't finished yet. They pledged their troth to each other, the memory of speaking the same words to Evan making her tear up unexpectedly.

It was only when Owen said quietly, "With this ring, I thee wed..." and pushed a simple silver ring over her knuckle to rest beside the gold band Evan had given her, that the enormity of what she'd done hit her.

She was married to Owen.

"I don't suppose you want to kiss her," Hollis drawled.

There was a faint flush high on Owen's cheeks.

"That's not necessary," she said fiercely.

Owen dropped her hands like her touch had burned him somehow.

"Pulling out in five," Hollis said. He'd tucked his Bible and prayer book beneath his arm and was already striding away.

And then August was there, slapping his brother's back. "Congratulations."

Owen shook his head as he stepped back. "Not necessary," he echoed her words from moments ago. One hand idly came up to rub his opposite biceps, where she knew he had a bullet wound beneath the sleeve of his shirt.

She was distracted when August swept her into a hug, his hands at her shoulders in a respectable way. She'd noticed that about him from the beginning. He was generous with his affection. A pat on the arm here, a hug for his adopted ward Ben, a young girl who'd been orphaned on the trail.

Owen was stingy with his touch. She'd never seen him embrace anyone.

Not that she wanted his touch. Or any man's.

When August let her go, he held her shoulders for a moment. "Come see me when my brother gets too bossy."

Felicity stepped close, but there was an uncertain moment, as if she didn't want to reach for a hug. Rachel had kept her distance from Felicity since August had made his preference for her clear.

Felicity stuck out her hand. "Congratulations."

Rachel shook it momentarily, finding a smile from somewhere. She wanted a moment alone. Wanted a wide bed in a bedroom that wasn't rolling across the prairie, a room with real walls. Wanted to curl up and let her muddled emotions find release.

But the bugle blew from not far away, blasting her ears. Her skin felt stretched too tight over her body. There was a rush of movement as stragglers rushed to put away their supplies. At the front of the company, the first wagon rolled into motion.

"Mason!" A male voice called out for Owen. As one of the captains of the company, he was often needed. Rachel should probably be glad that he hadn't been summoned in the few minutes it had taken them to wed.

He glanced over his shoulder at her, but she purposely tipped her chin in the other direction. He'd done enough for her this morning, hadn't he? Pushed his sister-in-law to get her breakfast, tracked down Hollis, married her.

August had disappeared, but Felicity hovered. What now?

The other woman offered a tentative smile. "I've got to track down Ben... would you want to come with me? Walk together today?"

Rachel guessed that August had put her up to it. He was a gentle soul who never wanted anyone to feel left out.

But the tightness in her lower back was a reminder that it was best not to be alone right now.

"Fine."

Two

RACHEL SAT on the bank of a little creek, half-hidden between a wild mulberry bush and something else with brambles. Women's voices filtered to her, their words muted by distance.

Her fingertips were stained red—her lips probably were, too, from the few berries she'd eaten. Her untied apron lay on the ground next to her. She'd made a small pile of mulberries and in a moment she would wrap them up and bring them back to camp with her.

Unlike the other women and girls who were moving easily through the woods seeking other bushes, Rachel had found this one laden with fruit and sat down.

Her lower back ached worse than it had when she'd woken up this morning. And for the past few minutes, she'd watched her stomach rippling beneath the fabric of her dress as her muscles tightened and released.

It was a strange sensation, just bordering on the edge of pain.

She'd felt it before, several nights ago. The strange

clenching of the muscles in her stomach. It had gone away then, so she expected it to fade in a bit. She wanted Mama, to ask what it meant. Glinda, her sister-in-law, had told Rachel some of what she'd experienced when Simon, Rachel's nephew, had been born. But Glinda was gone now, killed in the attack that had taken Evan's life, and Simon's too.

Rachel had no one to ask about the phantom pains that came and went.

For now, she tried to be grateful for the stolen chance to rest.

The days were slipping from springtime toward summer, which meant more hours each day the company could travel.

Hollis had driven them hard today. Almost fourteen miles. It was coming on evening and Hollis had called for the wagons to circle up as the women had found the berry patches and gone picking. It wouldn't be long before the others headed back to the wagons to make supper and care for their little ones.

Soon Rachel was going to have to face Owen. Her new husband.

Voices drifted through the woods, getting closer.

A particularly intense spasm moved through Rachel. She instinctively curled in to her stomach, her arm coming around her belly.

"...cold to me. I thought we'd become close—"

"Do you think she's keeping a secret?"

"I don't know—"

The voices cut off as a shadow fell over Rachel.

She glanced up to find Owen's sister, Alice, walking with Evangeline. Both using their aprons to carry mulberries, the material sagging from where they held them at their midsections.

She'd obviously surprised them with her presence, judging by Alice's wide eyes and Evangeline's sudden silence.

Rachel waited for the tightness in her belly to ease. Finally, she began to breathe easier.

Alice's sharp-eyed gaze pricked her. "What are you doing just sitting here?"

Not *are you all right?* or *do you need any help?*

"I'm fine, thank you," she said with a snap. "About to get up and return to camp."

Evangeline glanced around. The women who'd been in this area had slowly moved away, leaving Rachel mostly alone. And that was just fine with her.

"Do you... want us to wait?"

Rachel recognized Evangeline's hesitation and she'd seen Alice's lips purse, so she shook her head. "I'll be right behind you."

When Rachel had first been rescued by the company, Alice had been kind enough. She'd provided food for Rachel and Daniel, checked on Rachel often.

But they'd had an altercation after Daniel's death.

"You should be grateful for what my brother did," Alice *said.*

So righteous, with her nose upturned in the air.

And Rachel had been drowning in grief and fear. *"Your brother got my brother killed. If it weren't for Owen, Daniel would still be alive. Owen is a horrid, heartless man."*

They'd argued more, but Rachel couldn't recall the words she'd hurled in her grief-stricken state.

Alice had been cold to her ever since.

She knew Owen was close with his family. But she also hated the disdainful way Alice was looking at her now.

"Evangeline said you intend to marry my brother," Alice said stiffly.

Rachel had seen firsthand how quickly gossip could spread through the caravan of travelers. But Alice had it wrong. Somehow, she didn't know that Owen and Rachel had already married.

"Don't," Alice demanded.

Rachel clenched her left hand over the ring Owen had given her this morning. "I'll do what's best for me. And for Owen." She couldn't resist the dig, not with Alice looking at her as if she was a speck of dirt on her boot.

"You'd ruin his life?" Alice demand.

Evangeline looked as if she wanted to be anywhere else.

It was on the tip of Rachel's tongue to tell Alice it was already done, but another of the phantom pains came over her and stole her breath.

"We both know what you truly think about him," Alice said.

Rachel kept her face expressionless through the tightening of every muscle inside her.

"You're a selfish cow!" Alice cried.

She and Evangeline moved away, their voices going low so that Rachel couldn't hear what they said as they went. Alice sent one more look over her shoulder, unsmiling.

Owen would be unhappy when he found out about this.

Rachel sighed. She was angry with herself for losing her temper. She let her head drop back and looked up at the sky through the patchwork of tree limbs and leaf buds overhead.

It shouldn't matter that Alice didn't like her. But it rankled.

"She's so ugly."

The whisper from the past slithered through Rachel's mind, flooding her with memory.

"Look at her dress!"

Girlish giggles erupted from the back of the schoolroom. After several years of failed crops, Father had insisted the family move away from the homestead where Rachel had been born. They'd moved into the city, where Rachel had started at a new school. She'd left behind her closest friend, Beth, and the trio of girls her age had been unkind to her since she'd joined the classroom weeks ago.

Today was the first time they'd insulted her aloud.

The teacher didn't seem to notice.

When Rachel glanced over her shoulder, she saw their pointed glares. Tears smarted behind her eyes.

Daniel was her seatmate in the double desk and when he glanced at her, it was clear he'd heard, too. But he ducked his head over the slate in front of him.

"You should invite her to your birthday party next week," came the whisper from the third little girl.

For a moment, hope leaped in Rachel's chest.

But the first girl laughed. "Can you imagine? A pauper like her? She probably only has the one dress."

Rachel looked to the front of the classroom, but the teacher hadn't heard.

No one was going to help her, that much was clear.

She didn't need friends here, she thought fiercely. She had Beth.

She raised her hand and asked permission to use the privy outside. As she was walking by the girls' desk, she kicked over the lunch pail sitting at their feet.

A gasp erupted, but Rachel had put on an innocent smile. "I'm sorry. I didn't mean to be so clumsy."

It hadn't happened immediately, but the other girls had left her alone after she'd made it clear she wasn't a target for their cutting words.

She'd spent two lonely years in that school, keeping to herself, struggling with the arithmetic that her brother picked up so easily. She'd had no friends until Evan's family had moved into town. He'd joined their classroom when she'd been eleven, and everything had changed.

The spasm in her stomach passed, and Rachel blinked. She watched the two women leave the dappled woods and enter the fading sunlight.

She refused to beg or charm her way into Alice's good graces. Alice didn't know about the wedding yet, but maybe knowing Owen had married Rachel would soften Alice.

If it didn't... well, it was no matter. Rachel could survive on the harrowing trail without a friend.

It was awkward, trying to get up off the ground with her big belly and the cumbersome skirts tangling with her feet.

She'd almost caught her balance when a nudge from behind sent her to her knees. She landed painfully, her left foot twisting under her.

"You don't belong in this company." The woman's voice was unfamiliar but when Rachel looked up, she recognized Mrs. Bosworth.

Her husband had been the most adamant that Daniel be hanged. Daniel had stolen—and lost—their horse, and Mr. Bosworth had been unforgiving of the theft.

Rachel struggled to her feet, her mouth was already open to snap at the other woman. But Mrs. Bosworth stomped her foot—right on the mulberries Rachel had left lying on her apron on the ground.

There was an audible squish of the berries breaking, though several rolled away.

"You'll make yourself scarce if you know what's good for you."

The woman disappeared among the brush deeper in the woods, leaving Rachel trembling and her heart pounding.

That had sounded like a threat.

Useless arguments roiled in Rachel's throat. She hadn't been the one to steal Mr. Bosworth's horse. Her brother had been injured, afraid, desperate.

And wrong.

She'd known it the entire time. It was wrong of Daniel to steal that horse.

But he was her brother. He'd been the only person left in her life, such as it was, even though their relationship had been difficult for her entire life. She wasn't even sure she liked him. But he'd been hers.

And he was gone now.

She gathered up the apron with shaking hands. There were still some berries undamaged, but the mulberry juice would stain. Anger surged through her veins as she picked her way out of the woods.

With each step, pain shot up through her lower back and down her left thigh. Had she pulled something when Mrs. Bosworth had shoved her down? What had possessed the woman to bump into a pregnant woman? Did she have no decency?

Rachel's anger turned toward Evan. It was ridiculous, and she knew it. Her husband was dead. There was no use being angry at him now. But it was Evan who had sent them on this journey. Evan who had been overcome with excitement and wouldn't be talked out of it. Evan who'd told her in a commanding voice that he was the head of the household and he'd decided that they would go.

The wagons had circled not far across the rocky prairie field. A group of men rode off on horseback–hunting?

Another man approached on foot. She recognized the confident stride before it registered that it was Owen.

"What's the matter?" he demanded when he neared.

He always took that tone with her. Demanding. Bossy.

With her temper already ignited, his tone only fanned the flames.

"Why would anything be the matter?" she responded.

"You look..." He hesitated for the barest second and then waved his hand up and down to encompass her from head to toe.

She waited.

"What?" She put a demand in her voice, too, when he didn't finish his sentence.

He stood still. She kept walking.

"I don't know." He fell into step beside her. "Upset? Tired? Unhappy?"

She whirled on him, losing her grip on the mulberries. The apron fluttered to the ground, the remaining berries bouncing in every direction.

"I am unhappy," she snapped. "I never wanted to travel this trail. I want to go home."

He bristled, and she knew he was getting ready to argue with her.

And right now she couldn't take it.

She whirled and limped off, grateful when he didn't follow.

* * *

Later that night, Owen unsaddled his mount outside the circle of wagons, trying to pretend he wasn't spying on August.

The sun was setting, and August was supposed to be getting ready to ride out on watch, but there wasn't a lot of saddling going on yards away.

Maybe Owen's exhaustion was making him irritable.

Felicity fastened something near August's saddle bag, while August tugged on the simple bow that tied behind her waist.

From here, Owen couldn't tell what his brother was saying, but it was clear from the tilt to August's mouth, that he was teasing his new wife.

Owen dropped his left arm, releasing the buckle he'd held. The wound in his arm ached, and he flexed his fist. The pain was less than it had been yesterday. Tomorrow it'd be negligible. He was healing.

His eyes were drawn back to his brother, where Felicity turned as August caged her in with his arms. She raised one hand to thump his chest, but August only leaned into her and stole a kiss.

Owen looked away. Something about the private moment knotted his gut. He quickly picketed his horse and left them to their moment. August was responsible. He'd report for watch duty soon enough.

But Owen couldn't stop thinking about the pair as he walked toward the circle of wagons, absently rubbing the muscle just beneath his wound. He never would've chosen Felicity for his brother. She was shy and steady while August loved to chat and was constantly bringing people together.

Owen had pushed Rachel toward his brother, until

August had taken a stand and told Owen he had feelings for Felicity.

Owen had been... not angry. Only frustrated with August for keeping his feelings to himself for so long.

Owen might be used to being in charge, but he wanted what was best for his brother. And watching August and Felicity together showed him that his brother had obviously made the right choice.

You'll just throw her away? Like Pa did to us?

Leo's words from this morning echoed in his mind. He hadn't seen his brother all day. Was Leo still angry over Owen's decision?

He braced himself as he strode into camp, but it was Alice who was waiting for him near the fire. She had a plate of food in hand and got up to give it to him.

He took it with a quiet, "thank you." Past Alice, he caught sight of Rachel, who'd bedded down in her bedroll with her back to the fire.

This afternoon, when he'd come upon her walking alone toward camp, she'd looked tired. And sad. He hadn't been prepared for the kick in his gut, the worry, her expression had caused him.

She'd told him off, and he'd let her go rather than fighting.

She shifted now as he shoveled food in his mouth.

Other people had tents or slept in their wagons. He and August had started this journey sharing their wagon, sleeping under the stars. But when August and Felicity had married, Owen had left the wagon and its security to them. He hadn't thought he'd need it. A bedroll was enough for him.

But he had someone else to think about now.

"Did Rachel get dinner?" he asked.

Alice had turned toward the fire again, and he almost missed when she pulled a face. What was that about?

She turned toward him and propped her fists on her hips. "Don't marry her," she said urgently. "She's a troublemaker."

He thought he caught a flash of movement from the corner of his eye. Had Rachel twitched in her bedroll?

"We're already married," he told Alice calmly. "This morning."

"Owen, no! She's using you." Alice glared at the sleeping Rachel.

Her words were an unexpected slap—just like Leo's had been this morning.

Owen didn't understand. Alice liked everyone. She was well-liked in camp. He hadn't heard an inkling of her having a problem with Rachel.

He didn't like the pull between family and the choice he'd made, but he masked it and pretended she hadn't said anything. "I'd appreciate your making her feel welcome."

Alice wrinkled her nose.

"She needs our help," he said.

"She needs a switch to her backside. She's rude."

"So's Coop."

She looked taken aback at his quick retort. He hadn't argued with Alice once since he'd shown up on her doorstep in New Jersey. He was used to Leo pushing back, arguing with him. Not Alice.

He didn't like the way this felt, the way she was looking at him, as if he was a stranger to her.

"Alice, I'm not joshing. She's my wife now." He said the words with a quiet seriousness. He'd taken vows. He had a duty to Rachel for the foreseeable future. "Can I count on you?"

Alice shook her head and left the circle of light thrown by the flickering fire, leaving him to finish his food alone.

It tasted like ash in his mouth now. He couldn't have known that marrying Rachel would form a rift between him and Alice and Leo. But would knowing it have changed his mind? The weight of the guilt he carried hadn't shifted. He owed it to Rachel to see her to safety. Why couldn't his family understand?

Three

HOLLIS TREMBLAY SAT on a stump near a small trickle of a creek. He'd lathered up soap and now used a straight razor to shave. This was Hollis's third trip across the Oregon Trail and he'd learned that the folks in the caravan seemed to trust him more when he was clean-shaven rather than with a jaw full of whiskers.

A low-grade pain pulsed behind his left eye, but he staunchly ignored it. He'd had the same pain for weeks now. Ever since the storm. The pain did grow more faint, but it never went away. He swiped the straight razor on a towel laid over one leg, clearing away suds and whiskers.

He glanced down at the small, leather-bound notebook lying open on the ground at his left side. June sixteenth. He'd used a twig to hold open the book—its pages soft and a little fragile after two trips and much re-reading.

No, he was wrong. Today was June nineteenth. He was missing three days.

He scowled as he tipped his head back toward the sky,

running the straight razor under the angle of his chin. His eyes were unfocused on the blue sky overhead.

He scrambled to remember yesterday and the path they'd traversed. It came to him in snatches: riding horseback alongside his wagon, driven by a young man he'd hired in Independence. An antelope bounding across the plain, clearly startled by the noise of their wagons. He'd eaten supper—hadn't he? What about the day before?

Trying to force his brain to remember was like trying to hold water in a sieve. The harder he tried to grasp the memories, the more quickly they slipped out of reach. And the stronger the pain behind his eye.

He wiped his blade for the last time and then flipped the towel to a clean corner to give the blade a final cleaning. He folded the razor and slipped it into his pocket, then used the towel to clear his face of any remaining lather. He scooped up the book from the ground and ran his finger under the lines he'd written, a log of last year's journey. For this summer's trip, he was following along by the day and marking where there were differences in the miles traveled or where they made camp. They were currently twenty miles behind last year's journey.

"I can remember almost every moment of last year's journey, but I can't remember whether I've had breakfast today," he grumbled quietly to himself.

The twisting of his stomach seemed to indicate that he hadn't eaten yet this morning. The sun was well over the horizon now, and they needed to be pulling out soon. He could make up twenty miles over the next two weeks as long as they didn't have any long delays—like when the caravan had been hit by a tornado. Hollis had been lost from the wagon train for almost three days.

He couldn't remember the storm at all, though his most trusted captains had told him more than once how things had unfolded. Owen and August, the scout for the wagon train, believed Hollis had been attacked and bludgeoned in the head. That's where all his memory problems were coming from. At least he wasn't dizzy all the time anymore. And those first days after the storm, it had been impossible for him to sit a horse because the motion had made him sick to his stomach.

He tucked the journal safely in his hip pocket after tying it up with a bit of leather thong. He squatted at the trickle of water, splashed it on his face, and dabbed it dry with the towel. Most folks from the caravan would be visiting the deeper creek to wash dishes or clothes or even themselves. Hollis had chosen this tiny tributary to have some privacy.

"Just keep going," he told himself. Was he getting too old for this? He was only twenty-eight. He could go home...

He instantly clamped a lid on that thought. Too many broken dreams left behind.

He was still muttering to himself when he finally stood.

"You got a minute?"

He had heard the footsteps on rocky ground a half second before the man's voice reached his ears. Hollis faced August, who must have come from the direction of camp.

Hollis was a fine tracker in his own right, but August was on another level. The man could move silently through the prairie and had surprised Hollis into drawing his weapon a couple times after the head injury. He'd taken to announcing his arrival. Had August heard Hollis talking to himself?

August's expression gave nothing away. No hint of whether or not he had overheard. "I told Owen this morning, but I thought I should inform you too. I've been seeing wolf tracks."

"That's not uncommon in these parts," Hollis said. He had a notation in his journal that said they'd spotted a pack of wolves a little farther along the trail last summer.

"This pack seems to be following us," August said. "One of the wolves has a specific footprint."

Hollis gave the man his best impassive stare. He hadn't told anyone about his memory issues. He needed the people on the wagon train to trust him, and they wouldn't do that if they thought he couldn't lead them.

It was possible August had brought up the wolves to him in the past few days and Hollis couldn't remember.

"What do you want to do?" August said after a few moments.

"Tell the cowboys to be on alert." He had never had a run-in with wolves before. The animals were usually shy and didn't attack.

"I'd like to have Owen and the other captains ask the families with young children to keep them close," August said.

A beat of relief hit low in Hollis's stomach. This must be the first time August had brought it up. The headaches had improved. He could only hope that the problems with his memory would do the same before someone noticed.

August took his leave, and Hollis grabbed up his towel from where it had fallen into the bank. He walked back to camp determined to find some jerky or hardtack to tide him over until the evening.

A hymn wafted to him on a gentle breeze. Someone was singing. He recognized the tune from his childhood. His mother sang that song when she did chores like sweeping out their house or scrubbing laundry. A pang of homesickness moved through him before he pushed it away. It was easier if he didn't think about the people he'd left back home, especially the ones buried in the cemetery down the street from his parents' home.

As he reached camp, he realized there was no way to skirt around the singing woman at the wagon next to his, not when it was so close to time to pull out. Abigail was hitching up the oxen. The pale blue dress she wore contrasted with her dark brown hair and light brown skin. The ox only inches away was several times bigger than her, and Hollis recognized the ornery look in the animal's eyes.

He strode in her direction.

As she lifted the heavy yoke, the oxen shook its huge bony skull, coming dangerously close to knocking Abigail in the head. Her song cut off.

"Watch out!" Hollis nudged her with his hip and grabbed the singletree and slipped in the metal ring to secure it together. Abigail had stumbled a couple steps away, so she hadn't been knocked to the ground.

Thank goodness.

"What did you do that for?" she demanded with dark eyes flashing. It was a shock to hear that tone in the voice that had been singing so sweetly only moments ago.

"You shouldn't be hitching the animals by yourself. You could get hurt."

She frowned at him with a stormy look, unusual for her. "Who do you think has been hitching them up these past weeks?" She put her hands on her hips. "The only one giving me trouble around here is you."

She squinted at him. "Do you have a headache?"

"I'm right as rain," the white lie slipped out. He didn't like having to do it, but if she tried to order him to ride in a wagon, the way she had for the first few days after his accident, everyone would see him as weak.

"Did you eat anything for breakfast?"

"If I had known you'd be this much trouble, I would never have agreed to take you on," he said.

Her eyes flashed again. "You'll be rid of me soon enough. As soon as we get across the mountains."

Another traveler called his name. Hollis glanced over her shoulder.

First he had to get them all across the mountains. But he didn't know how he was going to do that if he didn't get his memory straightened out.

The next day, Owen was on horseback after guiding the lead wagon and several others to circle up. After weeks on the trail, folks knew what to do. The rest of the wagons had driven into place within the last half hour.

He'd ridden through and around camp, making sure everyone was settling in for the night.

Until he'd realized his wife was nowhere to be found.

The setting sun cast a golden glow over the prairie, but it only exacerbated his annoyance. Or maybe it was the faint pulsing pain in his arm. He'd hoped he wouldn't feel the wound at all today, but maybe he'd overdone it when he'd helped Mr. Johnson repair a broken spoke in his wagon wheel.

Where was Rachel? She knew better than to wander off by herself.

He approached Leo and Coop, who were out of the

saddle but standing with their two horses near where Leo's small herd of cattle was spread out in a loose bunch. Two cowboys on horses rode around the perimeter at a slow walk.

"You seen Rachel?" Owen called out.

He intended the words for Leo, but it was Coop who answered. "Can't keep track of your own wife?"

"Shut up."

"Don't talk to him like that," Leo growled.

Owen felt the verbal blow for what it was. His horse sensed his agitation, taking a step to the side. Leo was irritated with him, but they were family. Owen had expected his older brother to respect the decision he had made, even if Leo didn't agree with it.

He held onto the dregs of his patience. Reminded himself of the goal here. Find Rachel. Make up with his family. "I'll ride out with the herd tonight," like he'd done dozens of times during the journey so far, "but I want to make sure Rachel gets settled first."

Leo hiked his chin up stubbornly. "Don't bother. Sounds like you need to do some work managing your new household."

Coop snorted, hiding the sound and smile in his shoulder.

Owen felt his temper stir. "You're still angry with me."

Leo's eyes glinted like chips of ice when he swung his gaze on Owen. "What do you care?"

This wasn't the Leo who Owen had grown close to during the arduous journey. This was the man who'd opened the door back in New Jersey and then shut it in Owen's face. The man shaped by bitterness.

Righteous anger stirred in Owen's gut. He'd done so

much for his brother and sister—and this is how he was repaid?

"Alice is unhappy with you," Leo continued with a grim expression. "Maybe you should talk to her."

"I will talk to her, but right now I'm talking to you. August and I traveled across the country to find you, to make things right—"

"I'm not some child that needs a nursemaid."

Owen's eyes skipped to Coop of their own accord. The other man hadn't faced him directly this entire time, opting to fiddle with his saddlebags instead.

Coop had been in a heap of trouble when Owen and August had arrived in New Jersey. They'd found the family scrambling for a solution to their troubles—and the inheritance Owen had delivered had paid their way out here, onto the Oregon Trail.

Leo *had* needed him.

Coop swung into the saddle and rode off, hailing one of the other cowboys as Owen watched.

Leo must've followed Owen's thoughts, because a frown twisted his mouth.

"You asked for my help," Owen started. He wanted to patch this up.

"Maybe I don't need it anymore."

Maybe I don't need you. Owen heard the words as if Leo had uttered them aloud.

Hoofbeats pounded the ground. Owen looked over his shoulder to see August approaching. Relief swirled. At the interruption, at seeing his brother and closest friend in the world.

"You seen Rachel?" he called out before August had come near. He couldn't forget why he'd ridden out here.

"That's why I came looking for you," August sounded out of breath. "Felicity and Abigail said they hadn't seen her in a couple of hours."

Leo muttered something Owen couldn't hear.

The worried creases in August's face made Owen's gut tighten. "There were more wolf tracks just this morning."

That made... six sightings?

"Same ones?" Owen asked.

August nodded.

Owen thought about how slow Rachel moved carrying her baby in her stomach. The knot in his gut tightened further.

"Should I gather a search party?" August asked.

He'd included Leo in the question, his gaze encompassing both brothers. Leo was a captain in the company, too, and August seemed oblivious to the tension in the air. He was asking advice of two leaders.

"Not yet," Owen said. "I'm going to ride east." The trail they'd already traversed today. Could she be lagging behind?

"Want me to ask around some more?" August asked.

Leo remained silent, angry.

"Give me a few minutes," Owen said, grateful for his brother's quick thinking. "I'll find you."

He pushed his horse into a trot and then a gallup, back the way they'd come. Rachel knew better than to lag behind the group—their safety came from sticking together.

On the heels of that thought, he began to wonder whether marrying her was a mistake. He'd thought he would be able to smooth things over with Leo after the words his brother had hurled at him the morning of his marriage. *There's nothing honorable in what you're doing.*

But it'd been two days and his brother was still riled up. And Alice was upset, too.

Owen had tried to do right by Rachel. Of anybody, he'd thought Leo might understand. Leo had stepped in to help Evangeline when her father had been injured in a river crossing. This wasn't any different, except for the ring Rachel was wearing.

What was Leo's problem?

He hadn't ridden far when he caught sight of a solitary figure trudging toward him. Rachel.

The beat of relief was quickly eclipsed by irritation. Leo's words still ringing in his ears, he reined in and jumped off his horse to approach her on foot for the last several yards.

"Where have you been?" he demanded. "You know it's dangerous to be so far behind the caravan."

One hand curled around her belly; her lips formed into a scowl. "I'm not that far out of sight."

His brows jumped on his forehead. "Not far, huh? The wagons have all circled up for the night. And you're still walking." He threw one arm behind him to indicate the wagons, still out of sight.

She blew out an audible breath, stuttered a step and then stopped.

Was she trying to make him angry?

"Are you hungry?" she bit out. "Did you need me to make your supper? Is that it?"

"There have been wolf tracks close to camp. August has seen tracks from the same pack more than once."

He saw her flinch. Saw the stubborn way she pressed her lips together just before she opened them to speak again.

"You shouldn't be alone out here," he said. "Especially after dark."

"How am I supposed to know about the danger," she panted a breath. "If you don't tell me?"

The woman was going to irritate him to his grave. "Come *on*," he grunted.

At the very moment the words left his lips, he registered the way she was standing, with her shoulders tense and hand protectively over her belly. He'd thought her tension was directed at him, but this... it looked as if she was focused inside her body.

As if she was in pain.

"Are you having labor pains?" He took a few steps forward, until he was towering over her. He reached for her elbow, but she tugged out of his grasp, exhaling a noisy breath as she did.

"I'm fine." She stood taller, body relaxing. She started walking in the direction Owen had come from.

He'd left his horse standing where he'd dismounted, and Rachel skirted the animal.

Owen kept pace with her, gathering the horse's reins as he passed. Pain flared momentarily in his arm and then faded.

"Whatever that was, it didn't look fine."

She didn't answer him. Didn't even look his direction.

"That's why you'd fallen behind. Labor pains." His brain whirled, trying to figure out what to do next. Get Maddie? Start hauling water from the creek?

"Get on the horse," he told her.

She sent him a scathing look. "I won't."

He let his eyes rove her head to toe. She couldn't be that heavy. He could carry her. It wasn't far to camp.

She frowned fiercely at him, as if she'd heard his thoughts. "It's false labor pains. I've been having them for almost a week. They come and go."

For a week? And she hadn't told anyone?

"You should've told me," he snapped. "How am I supposed to help you if I don't know—"

"You mean you don't like having information withheld?" She tossed the words at him. "Like the fact that wolves might be hunting our company?"

"They aren't hunting our company." Exasperation leaked out. "They're likely scavenging scraps that have been left behind. And Hollis didn't want to set everyone in camp in a panic." Things were more difficult when folks were fearful or panicked. Mistakes were made, people got hurt.

"If you want my help, you need to trust me—"

She interrupted before he was finished. "When have you given me reason to trust you?"

The moment when he'd pulled her up on his horse as a horde of buffalo had stampeded toward them flashed through his memory. He'd saved her life.

"Right now," he said quietly, hoping she would hear the seriousness behind them. "If we're going to make it to the Willamette Valley, we've got to work together."

She gave him a long considering glance. She didn't argue as they walked silently toward camp.

But he couldn't help noticing she hadn't answered back.

"Have any more of those labor pains?"

Two days had passed since Owen had found out about her phantom pains. The man had been hovering ever since, at least when his duties as captain didn't pull him away.

Rachel glanced up to Owen. He was only inches away, though he was standing while she was sitting with her legs out in front of her and her back against a wagon wheel. Evening was falling, the sky a deep blue over the sparse vegetation of the area.

He held a plate in his extended hand and she took it, careful not to unbalance it. "None," she said quietly.

She expected him to step away, but instead he shifted an empty crate from nearby onto its side and perched on top of it. Which meant he sat right next to her.

When Hollis had called for the halt tonight, Owen had been on horseback and found her walking alongside some of the other women as the wagons started to circle. He'd dismounted and walked with her, leading his horse.

She'd heard the whispers his actions had caused, though he hadn't made any indication that he'd noticed.

In camp, the wagon he and August shared wasn't in its usual spot next to Leo and Evangeline's two wagons. He'd moved into position between Collin and Stella's wagon and the wagon helmed by Abigail and Felicity.

Leo and Evangeline, along with Alice and Coop, were sticking close to their campfire. Avoiding Owen? Or Rachel?

Owen had spent the past hour cooking supper with Collin Spencer's wife, Stella, and her sister Lily Fairfax. The third Fairfax sister, Maddie, was elsewhere in the camp, checking on a young boy who'd recently suffered a bad burn. Rachel had spent a lot of time watching people since she'd come into this company, and she was envious of the close relationship shared by Stella and her sisters. She'd been close with Glinda, had that special connection where they'd known each other's hurts and sorrows, shared joys and warmth.

There was no use in being envious. She tried to stuff the feeling away, aware of Owen sitting quietly beside her.

Maybe she'd been especially hungry this evening, but the

baby seemed to enjoy the simple venison and fry bread. The baby kicked little taps into Rachel's side, the movements from inside tickling her until she laid her hand flat on that spot.

"The baby all right?" Owen's words, spoken around the bite in his mouth, were unexpected.

He'd been quiet yesterday and this evening. It unnerved her. She'd grown used to the man who argued constantly and ordered her around.

"He or she seems to like the supper you cooked. The baby is either learning to dance or practicing to play stick ball."

Some fine tension eased off his forehead. He frowned at his plate. "You sure those muscle spasms or labor pains or whatever they are aren't dangerous?"

She'd just scooped another bite into her mouth and now chewed and swallowed before she tried to answer. "I've never done this before," she said quietly, aware of Collin and Stella across the fire. "My mother is hundreds of miles behind us. I can't ask her. And I won't—"

She'd started to say she wouldn't ask any of the older women on the wagon train, but she held back the words.

A dark shadow hovered behind Owen's eyes when he glanced at her next. Did he sense the bitterness inside her?

He always bossed her around. Would he tell her to stop dwelling on it?

She braced for a terse command, her lips already twisted, ready to refute whatever it might be. But he tapped the edge of his fork on the edge of his plate and didn't look at her when he said, "I don't remember my ma having those kinds of pains. I was eleven when she carried her last baby."

The rising steam inside her vanished at his unexpected words.

"Do you miss her?" She didn't know where the words

48

came from, but there they were, hanging between them in a suddenly awkward silence.

He didn't answer directly. "She died before the baby was born." There was a tightness in his voice. He squinted into the fire.

And then he turned his intense gaze on her. "Who do you want to help you, when the time comes?"

It took a moment for his words to register. When the baby came. That's what he meant.

"I don't know," she answered honestly. Now it was her turn to jerk her gaze away, to stare unseeingly at her empty plate. "I had planned for my sister-in-law to help me." She swallowed the sudden lump in her throat.

Since the attack, Rachel had avoided thinking about the baby's arrival. She and Glinda had spoken about it in general terms and planned for what supplies they would need when the baby came. It was assumed that Glinda would help. They'd both known it. Evan would have stayed out of it, unless she'd asked specifically for his help. Not that he would've said no. Evan could be like her father sometimes. He'd believed that a woman's work was a woman's, and a man's work was a man's.

He'd never cooked supper, like Owen had tonight.

She thrust that thought away.

There was no comparing Evan to Owen. Evan had loved her.

Owen had married her as a convenient solution for both their problems.

Owen cleared his throat. "Did you and your husband have names picked out? For a boy or girl?"

A wave of emotion crashed over her, tightening her

throat. She didn't want Owen to talk about Evan. Evan was hers, and she wouldn't share him.

"You don't need to waste your time coddling me," she said angrily, though she kept her voice low, aware of the trio conversing across the fire.

She saw the surprise in his expression when he threw a sharp glance at her, the way his brows drew together to make his expression stormy.

The sound of a jaunty whistle approached. She glanced away from Owen, but not before she saw the muscle jumping in his cheek.

A single tear slipped down her cheek and she brushed it away, praying he hadn't noticed.

August entered the circle of firelight, his arms full of what looked like several folds of a canvas cover from one of the wagons.

"This what you wanted?" He addressed the question to Owen, who nodded.

August deposited the bundle that overflowed his arms onto the ground at Owen's feet. Owen set aside his empty plate. "Thanks."

August tipped his hat to Rachel. "Fine evening, isn't it? Your feet hurting?"

She'd barely shifted, but August was incredibly good at noticing fine details.

"Only from the moment I wake up until I fall asleep." She'd started loosening the laces of her boots around her sixth month. Now even the toes pinched constantly. She'd kicked off her boots when they'd settled in camp. The rocky soil in this area wasn't the best for going barefoot, but she couldn't bear the boots any longer tonight.

August tipped his head to Maddie, who'd joined her

sisters, while Collin had disappeared. "Maddie might have something you could soak your feet in."

That would mean she'd have to track down a tub—and beg to borrow it—and haul water, heat it...

Just the thought of it made Rachel feel even more weary. And sad. She'd had two tubs in the wagon she'd shared with Evan. They were lost to her now. Now she had nothing.

She pinched her lips together when they wanted to tremble. "I'll be all right. Thank you for thinking of me."

August and Owen shared a speaking glance before August excused himself and disappeared back the way he'd come, leaving her with the awkward silence and her husband.

Owen nudged the canvas with the toe of one boot.

"What is that for?" She couldn't keep her curiosity from spilling out in the words. She hadn't noticed anyone with a torn canvas today. Was he repairing it?

"My new sister-in-law has a habit of collecting items that might be useful along the trail. I think she took this off an abandoned wagon a couple of days ago."

What was *he* doing with it?

"I asked her if I could have it. With the right supports and some stakes and string, I can craft a tent for you."

You don't need to waste your time coddling me.

The words she'd thrown at him moments ago rang in her ears. They sounded both childish and ungrateful. She couldn't have known that he meant to do *this*.

She waited for him to stand up and walk off. Say something like *You don't deserve it.*

Walking off in a fit of temper was something Daniel would've done. He'd learned it from their father. Evan would've been quieter about making his displeasure known.

Owen moved, and she flinched. She tried to hide the

instinctive reaction by shifting her legs. She didn't know whether he'd noticed.

He pulled the top of the canvas up, stretching it out between his arms. "Might have to cut and sew it back together to get the right shape. A tent is different than the curved top of the wagons."

His voice was even, though he wasn't looking at her.

Until he did. "It isn't four walls, but you and the baby will want some privacy until we reach Oregon."

Suddenly, the hot lump in her throat wasn't about missing Evan and Glinda and Simon. Owen had remembered her words from days ago, how she longed to be back in a house.

Stella walked around the fire toward them, clearly collecting plates.

Rachel lumbered off the ground because it was easier than staying near Owen. When he would've protested her taking his plate and spoon, she said, "I'll help Stella with the dishes."

He held her gaze for a long moment but didn't argue.

As she knelt on the bank of the creek in the dark, her mind wouldn't stop spinning.

She didn't know why Owen had shown this kindness toward her.

It bothered her. What did he want in return?

But she also couldn't deny that she was secretly relieved. Enough so that silent tears joined the creek water bubbling down the stream.

Four

OWEN WAS up before the sun, as were a few other travelers. It was that quiet time before even the birds woke. The sky was clear and a blanket of stars shone above him like sparkling diamonds.

He hadn't gotten as far as he wanted on Rachel's tent last night. He had taken some measurements of the canvas and promised himself to look for some tall, straight saplings for tent poles as they crossed more miles today. She'd been just as prickly as ever last night, and he wasn't sure why he bothered. Especially after his confrontation with Leo.

Was taking care of Rachel worth this rift in his family?

It didn't help that a tiny voice deep inside him wondered whether Leo had been watching and waiting for something—anything—to distance himself from Owen. He'd been insistent from the beginning that he didn't want or need another brother.

Owen fed the fire small twigs, getting it back to a level where the women could cook breakfast. Then he pulled on his boots and rolled up his bedroll. Rachel, in close proximity, stayed asleep.

Collin and Stella had curled together in their bedrolls underneath Stella's wagon last night, while Lily and Maddie slept in a tent nearby. It was still quiet enough that he heard the younger man stir.

No. Collin was the same age as Owen. He only seemed younger because Owen was used to playing older brother.

Collin murmured an apology to Stella. He must have woken her up.

"I'm fine," the barest whisper traveled through the morning air to Owen's ears. "It's not the gunshot wound, it's my shoulder. I must have slept on it wrong." Another little murmur that Owen couldn't make out followed by a soft hum made him wonder if he needed to make himself scarce. Then the rustling of fabric, as if Collin had shifted to his elbow in his bedroll.

"Maddie found it last night hidden in the bottom of the salt barrel," Stella whispered.

"What did she do?"

"She was angry. At first, she thought I'd lied to the soldiers back at that fort, but then I explained. Still..."

"She still wasn't happy about being kept in the dark," Collin finished the statement.

What were they talking about? Something that Maddie had found? Some secret Stella and Collin had kept from her?

Stella was an expert at keeping secrets. She had hidden her identity as a woman for almost a month on the trail. Collin had been the first one to discover the truth and had helped her carry on with the deception, trying to protect her and her sisters from some very bad men who were following them west.

Collin was besotted with Stella, but Owen had a hard time trusting someone who had lied to him once. Now Collin was keeping secrets too?

They must have registered that he was awake because they went silent.

Soon enough, Collin joined Owen by the fire, pulling his suspenders over his shoulders, his jaw cracking with a big yawn. Someone must have filled the coffee pot with water last night because Collin nestled it into the coals at the edge of the fire. Owen had tried to think of everything they would need on this journey, but he might have underestimated the amount of coffee his family would consume along the way.

Collin nodded toward the still sleeping Rachel. "She's a little easier to take when she's asleep."

Was that a joke? Owen didn't respond.

"Oh, come on," Collin murmured. "Everyone in the wagon train feels the same way."

Owen bristled.

He had a hard time getting along with Rachel. He knew others did, too. But part of him argued that Collin wasn't being fair. "She hasn't had a moment of peace since we found her frightened in the woods. She lost all her supplies. And her family."

Collin looked slightly abashed, but there was a stubborn set to his jaw.

"Maybe that'll change," Owen said, his eyes on the fire.

"What will?"

"How people think about her."

"Hmm." Collin didn't seem to agree. "Or maybe folks have long memories."

Owen frowned. He glanced to where Rachel still slept, only her fair hair visible above the edge of the bedroll.

"Are you going to stock up more supplies when we get to the fort?" Collin's question shook Owen out of uncharitable thoughts toward the other travelers.

"What do you mean?"

"Don't babies need diapers? Lots of clothes for when they mess them?"

Owen hadn't given a lot of thought to that. After the other day, when Rachel had been having those pains, he had been more focused on the imminent arrival of the baby. He knew she'd been putting up a small stash of things, that Felicity had helped her. But he didn't know whether it was enough.

The vows he had spoken in front of Hollis echoed in his mind. He'd promised to provide for Rachel. She'd come to this marriage with virtually nothing, and it was his duty to see she had all she needed. She hadn't asked him for anything, and she was stubborn enough that she might try to tough it out even though she didn't have the right supplies. He also knew that the trail ahead might take them through some terrain where water would be difficult to find. How was she going to wash out the baby's diapers then?

Maddie rushed into camp. Owen hadn't even noticed she had been gone. Had someone woken her in the night?

She made a beeline for Collin—no, she made a beeline for Owen. "The Schaefer family is in a bad way. John and Mary have been vomiting and worse all night."

His mind immediately went to work on the problem. The family had four small children, the oldest couldn't be more than five or six. "You think it's cholera?"

She shook her head. "I don't know. It could be something they ate."

"What do you need?"

"I already spoke to Hollis, and he says we can't afford to delay. If both of them are laid up in their wagon, who's going to drive it?"

"If the kids aren't ill, you need to keep them separated from their parents," Collin added seriously.

"I'll handle the children, you just concentrate on getting them well," Owen told Maddie.

"Don't let yourself get sick," Collin added.

Maddie shot him a squinty-eyed look, and Owen couldn't help remembering the conversation he'd overheard a few moments ago.

"Come back to the wagon and get some rest after we roll out," Collin said.

Maddie frowned at him. "I'll do what needs doing."

Collin's words about Rachel's reputation still hung at the back of Owen's mind. He had come to join her last night as the wagons circled up, staking his claim—or so he thought, by staying at her side all evening. But he hadn't made any announcement to the company at large. Alice hadn't known about the wedding until he'd told her.

Maybe if folks knew he'd married Rachel, they'd think more kindly toward her, though it might take more than that to repair her reputation in the company after everything that happened with Daniel.

What if helping a sick family could be a chance for Rachel to repair her reputation?

He crouched next to Rachel, hating to wake her. Until last night, he hadn't realized how restless she was when she slept. He'd woken several times in the night when she'd rolled over heavily. Was she uncomfortable with her bulging belly? Or was it more of those labor pains?

She probably wouldn't tell him if it was.

If he was truly going to help Rachel, that included helping her with her reputation.

He reached out and touched her shoulder, jostling her slightly. "Wake up."

She came to with a start, her arm flailing up. It was a fluke that the back of her hand cracked him right in the nose.

"Ow!" He went down onto his knees beside her, one hand prodding the now tender bulb of his nose.

Her eyes were wide, her breaths coming frantically fast.

"What are you doing?" she demanded, scrabbling backwards. She sat up, and one arm went protectively around her stomach. "Are you bleeding?"

"Stop looking at me like I am going to hurt you. You're the one who just punched me." He said the words from behind his hand and they emerged muffled.

"Why did you grab me like that?"

"I didn't grab you at all. I barely touched your shoulder."

Her eyes snapped at him and her mouth opened. They could be here arguing all morning if he didn't put a quick stop to this. He had to remember there were folks who needed their help.

"At our wedding ceremony, you promised to be my helpmate."

A wariness entered her eyes.

"There's a family who needs us today. I'm acting in my capacity as captain, and I need you to help me."

He figured it was better if he didn't mention anything about her reputation. He didn't want to give her any more reason to be frustrated at him this morning, even though the reputation she carried wasn't his fault in the least.

"I can't lift anything very heavy. And I don't move fast," she reminded him.

"I think it will mostly be wrangling the family's little kids. Their Ma and Pa are pretty sick."

She still didn't look convinced, and now the camp was well and truly waking up around them.

"I could really use your help," he said.

He saw the stubborn set of her jaw and braced for a refusal. But there was a slight softening to her frown, and she grudgingly said, "Fine."

He felt a beat of relief. "Take a few minutes to wash up. I'll scramble a couple of eggs and then we need to get over to their wagon ."

Rachel walked several paces out from the wagon.

She and Owen had gone to assist the Schaefer family and found Maddie caring for the mother and father, who were lying in their wagon bed.

It had only been a short time since the wagons had pulled out. Owen was walking next to the oxen pulling the wagon. The oldest boy, Fergus, who must have been all of seven, walked at Owen's side. Rachel couldn't hear what they were saying, but her eyes strayed to her husband.

She had been surprised when Owen had asked Maddie to help him wrap the eight-month-old baby in a way he'd seen some of the other mothers do, so that the blanket held the baby over his chest while he walked. This left Rachel with two little girls, ages two and four. Ethel and Margaret.

The two girls chattered like magpies, and Rachel found herself constantly swiveling her head, trying to make sure that neither one of them got close enough to the wagon that they would get run over. A wagon wheel could crush a hand or foot in an instant.

"You got a baby in there?"

Rachel looked down at Margaret, who had asked the impertinent question.

She couldn't fault her for curiosity. It had been one of the things that she had loved most about her nephew Simon. A streak of missing him went through her, and she quickly blinked it away as Ethel, the younger of the two, fell back a step.

"I do have a baby that will be coming soon," Rachel said.

"What are you gonna name it?"

Owen had asked her that, and she hadn't given him an answer. "I'm not sure yet."

"My brother's name is Fergus. If it's a boy, maybe you could name it Fergus."

Rachel gave a noncommittal hum and slowed down another step further when Ethel lagged behind.

"Keep up," Rachel encouraged. But then Ethel stopped completely.

"She don't like to walk," Margaret said in a matter-of-fact manner.

"Everything all right?" Owen called over his shoulder. He hadn't even turned to see.

"Fine," Rachel replied.

But no matter how she cajoled, Ethel wouldn't start walking again. Instead, she lifted her arms to Rachel.

"She wants you to carry her," Margaret said.

Somehow Rachel kept the huff of impatience from escaping. She scooped the girl into her arms. It was awkward, balancing her over the bulk of Rachel's belly.

She'd only gone a few steps when Owen turned to look.

He said something to Fergus and strode back toward her. "What do you think you're doing?"

The snap in his voice made irritation crawl beneath her skin, but there was also a tiny part of her that found humor in the way his face thunderclouded above the baby nestled against his chest.

"I am carrying this child, who insists she cannot walk another step."

Owen shook his head and reached for the girl as he neared, but Rachel turned her body away, so that the little one was out of reach. "You can't hold her and the baby too."

She saw the consternation move across his face—and the flicker of grudging agreement in his eyes when he recognized that she was right.

She nodded toward Fergus. "Should you really leave him in charge of the wagon?"

"I have to go," Margaret said.

When both Rachel and Owen looked at her, she opened her eyes even wider. "You know, go."

"Let me have Ethel," Owen said. He took Ethel from her arms and held her as if she was a downy pillow instead of a squirming little girl. Rachel saw the flex of his bicep as he settled her on his hip. "Take Margaret over to that little copse of trees for some privacy. Hurry back. If I stop the wagon now, we'll lag toward the back of the group, but we'll be all right."

Rachel did as he asked, Margaret keeping up a steady stream of dialogue, including her thoughts on the tiny yellow flowers dotting the landscape, the bluebird that they flushed out of the small group of scrubby evergreen trees, and whether it was going to rain again soon.

When they got back to the wagon, Rachel thought

Owen might reprimand her for taking too long, but it was hard to walk fast with her girth. He didn't. He had pulled the canvas cover of the wagon back from the first slat, so it stood open. He had climbed up on one of the spokes in the wagon wheel as he rummaged around inside the wagon. He must have heard them coming, thanks to Margaret's chatter.

"We're going to try something different," he said. "You and the kids ride in the wagon for now."

Rachel pulled a face.

He tipped his chin down and raised his brows. "What?"

"Won't they be bored?"

He sighed. "Leo let me borrow one of Evangeline's books. Maybe you can read to them and keep them occupied."

He handed Margaret up into the wagon seat so she could crawl over and join her brother and younger sister. From here, Rachel could see that he had rearranged the crates and boxes so there were some seats inside. He draped a quilt over one area and made a seat for Rachel too.

The baby started fussing where she was still tied to Owen's chest.

Margaret's head popped up over the edge of the wagon. "She might be crying because she's worried about Ma and Pa."

All of a sudden a baby wasn't the only one crying. Two big tears rolled down Margaret's cheeks.

Owen glanced at the last of the wagons that were rolling past. He seemed unruffled, swaying back-and-forth on his feet a little bit while jiggling the baby.

He stepped closer to the side of the wagon and reached his hand out, palm up. Margaret slipped her hand into his. He jiggled it a little and the touch seemed to break the little girl out of her emotional state.

"Your ma and pa are going to get better," he said reassuringly.

Rachel inhaled, opening her mouth too, but a sharp look over his shoulder silenced her.

"Miss Maddie is taking care of them, and making sure they get enough water and some broth. They just need to rest and in a few days, they'll have their strength back."

"What if we get sick?" Fergus asked.

Owen still didn't seem in any hurry to get moving again, not when the kids were upset, though the wagons rolling away made Rachel feel anxious.

"If you get sick, Miss Rachel and I will take care of you. But I don't think you're going to get sick."

"Can we check on Ma and Pa?" Margaret asked.

Owen tipped his head to the line of wagons moving ahead of them. "When we stop for lunch. As long as we don't get too far behind."

The kids went a little wide-eyed and moved quickly to settle in the wagon.

"Tum on, Miss Wachel," Ethel said.

Owen raised his brows, hand out to assist her into the wagon.

"Do you need me to take her?" Rachel nodded to the baby, still fussing.

"She's probably ready for a nap. She settled pretty good when I was walking. Let's leave her as she is and see if she'll doze off," Owen replied.

Fine.

Rachel ignored Owen's outstretched hand and grabbed the running board instead, putting one foot on the wagon wheel to boost herself up.

But her boot slipped and she lost her balance. Before she

could fall, Owen was there. She landed heavily against him, her arm going over his shoulder and her hip against his side.

One of her feet was still on the wagon wheel, and Owen bore all her weight.

"You all right?"

Her heart beat wildly, but not from his touch. It was because she had slipped. It had to be.

The baby gave a violent kick right where she was pressed up against Owen, and his eyes flew to her face.

"Was that—" He looked awed. It was the same wondrous expression Evan had worn the first time she'd put his hand on her belly so he could feel the baby move.

But Owen wasn't Evan, and this wasn't his baby. The hurt that squeezed her lungs made her unable to speak. She just nodded.

He boosted her into the seat, shooting another sideways glance at her. He made sure she was settled before he gave the oxen the command to keep moving.

She was grateful for the distance between them.

She found the book where he had tucked it near her seat and was surprised at how comfortable her seat was. Had Owen padded it?

The children were quiet for the moment, and she watched Owen as his hand came up to rest behind the baby's head. He was right. The baby had gone quiet after they had started walking.

Seeing him with the children, his compassion and care for them, reminded her of those moments when they'd joined Maddie at the Schaefers' wagon that morning. Owen had been reassuring as he told the parents that he was going to watch over the kids for the day, that he was going to take care of things. She'd seen the look of relief wash over the father's face, and Owen had been the cause of it.

She had known that he took his duties as captain seriously, but until today, she had only seen his command when he had been disciplining Daniel or leading the men against the bandits.

This was a softer side of him. If he had offered this side of himself to her from the beginning, would she feel differently toward him now?

Five

A GUSTY WIND had blown all night long. Now a fog covered the ground, along with a cool temperature. It was mid morning now, but it was still difficult to see the other travelers walking nearby. Even the wagon in front of Owen was a hulking shadow through the mist.

Mr. and Mrs. Schaefer were doing a little better today, but Maddie had asked him and Rachel to watch the children again, to give the husband and wife one more day to recover before they had to take over their duties on the trail. Two other families had experienced the same symptoms as the Schaefers, and it disquieted Owen.

Rachel hadn't spoken much this morning. He was a little worried that she was feeling ill, but her color was good.

He'd had the middle-of-the-night watch again last night, and she'd been restless when he'd left their campsite in the dead of night. When he'd returned well before dawn, he was fairly sure she'd been awake. She'd been too quiet, too still, to actually be asleep.

He'd thought about asking her if something was wrong, if

she was having more of those pains. But he hadn't. It seemed too awkward somehow. They weren't friends, even though they were husband and wife.

It would be a relief to finish her tent and have a little separation from her. She was currently taking up too much of his thoughts. It was easier to think of her in terms of tasks that needed to be done. Ways he could help.

Right now he could hear the cadence of her voice as she read to the Schaefer children in the wagon bed. He'd noticed the way she had stretched when she'd come out of the wagon last night, one hand resting at her lower back, as if she was hurting.

But she hadn't complained. About any of it.

He'd asked August to stay on horseback today, riding up and down the caravan this morning with the visibility so poor. Hoofbeats and his brother's voice calling his name jerked Owen out of his conflicting thoughts about his wife.

August reined in nearby. "Alice is in a bad way."

Owen snapped into a sharp focus. "What's the matter?"

"Maybe the same affliction that the Schaefers are suffering from. She can't seem to keep anything down."

"Is she lying in her wagon?"

August shook his head. "She keeps saying she can walk, but she's pale as a ghost and looks like a stiff wind might blow her over."

"Where's Leo?"

"He rode out with the cowboys this morning, looking for a couple of head that had strayed from the herd. Hollis asked me to take a count of everyone who's feeling poorly."

The noise from the wagon had gone quiet and a glance over his shoulder showed Owen that Rachel and little Margaret were watching. Listening.

"Can you drive the oxen for a bit while I check on Alice?"
he asked her.

"Help me down," was the answer he got. She started
moving toward the back of the wagon, where he could let her
down without halting the oxen.

He nodded to August, who rode off into the fog, and
rounded to the rear of the wagon. He was careful not to get
too close to the still turning wheels as he reached up for her.

"Put your hands on my shoulders," he instructed.

He saw the quick frown but she didn't argue—a miracle
in itself—and when her upper body fell against him with the
momentum of the rolling wagon, he took her weight easily.

He felt the press of her belly against his chest as she kicked
her legs over the tailgate, and for a beat of remembrance, he
felt a phantom kick like the one he'd felt when he'd caught
her yesterday.

He didn't know what to do with the shock of touch. "All
right?" he gruffed as he set her feet on the ground.

She inhaled deeply and for a moment her eyes were locked
on his, uncertainty in their depths.

She blinked and hid it from him. "I'm fine. But I don't
know how to drive oxen."

"Your husband never taught you?"

She shook her head, eyes gone sharp, like they did every
time the man came up in conversation.

"C'mere."

He made sure the children were contained in the wagon
—Fergus had taken over reading the pirate story, though he
was much slower than Rachel—and they seemed to be staying
out of trouble for the moment.

He led Rachel to where he'd been walking beside the
oxen. Her head only came up to his shoulder and he felt a

moment of misgiving, but the oxen were trained well. And Alice needed him.

"You'll want to keep that wagon in sight." He pointed ahead to where the top of the canvas cover of the wagon ahead was visible.

"This morning isn't ideal. It's difficult to see. You'll have to pay close attention."

"I can pay attention," she said with a tinge of exasperation in her tone. "How do I make them stop?"

He went over the commands for stop, go, left, right.

"You don't have to worry about these two," he said. "Except for Zeke, who pulls to the left. They know what their job is along this journey."

Her gaze flicked to the oxen just beyond him. Was that a beat of fear in her eyes?

He needed it gone. Animals could sense her temerity. "It's too bad children aren't trained like the oxen are. Or wives."

He caught the sharp flick of her eyes. There was a beat of stilted silence until he turned up one corner of his mouth.

She pursed her lips. "Don't you mean husbands?"

Now certain she would be all right, he jogged away, glancing over his shoulder once to catch a glimpse of Rachel through the stringy fog. She was turned away, maybe speaking to one of the children in the wagon.

He kept going. With the children's needs slowing them down, they'd fallen more toward the back of the company. Alice and Leo's wagon was toward the front.

He didn't like the weather. The low visibility meant more chance of coming up on a gully or even a muddy place or badly rutted part of the trail. The last thing the company needed was to wreck one of the wagons or have someone injured due to inattention.

He found Alice a few paces behind her wagon, the oxen still pulling. She was bent over with her hands on her knees, retching.

She'd straightened by the time he jogged the last few yards to reach her, then wiped her mouth with the back of her hand.

"You should be lying down," he chided.

She waved him off, half-turned like she wanted to spare him from seeing her.

He detoured to the back of the wagon where a pail hung off the side. He pulled a dipper of water from inside and trekked back to her.

She was still standing where she'd been, looking shaky on her feet. Another wagon emerged from the fog behind, looking like a mysterious pirate ship, one Rachel might've been reading about.

Owen put his arm around Alice's waist and moved his sister out of the wagon's path.

"Drink this," he said.

Worry kicked in his gut. What if this sickness spread throughout the entire caravan?

A muffled groan split the air.

Rachel ladled a thin broth out of the cookpot and into a tin bowl.

The entire caravan was quiet tonight. The usual sounds of cooking and chatter were subdued. Several more families had fallen ill, and when Owen had passed through earlier, he'd told Rachel that Hollis was thinking of taking tomorrow as a rest day to see if it would help. Hollis had also insisted every family boil the water used for drinking or cooking. Rachel didn't know how that would help, but Hollis was to be obeyed.

She took the bowl of broth to Alice, who lay in her tent with the flap open. She had a slop bucket nearby and had raced out of the tent and off into the woods a couple of times already.

She looked pale and shaky and turned her face away when Rachel approached. "I don't want any food," she whispered, voice raspy.

Rachel wouldn't soon forget the way Alice had spoken to her days ago, but it was clear the other woman needed help.

"Owen said you should try to drink some of this. You need to keep your strength up."

Alice shook her head, her hair tousled on the pillow. One hand clutched her stomach over the blankets raised to her waist.

"I can't," she whispered brokenly.

"Owen said—"

Alice's eyes flashed angrily. "Owen isn't my keeper, and you aren't either. Go away."

Rachel edged back. She didn't want Owen to return and find Alice weak from hunger. But arguing with the woman wasn't going to get anywhere either.

"I'll leave it for you. In case you change your mind."

Alice only closed her eyes.

Rachel whirled and walked back to the fire. She'd go check on Mr. and Mrs. Schaefer and the children. They had been sitting up—although still pale and moving gingerly— when she'd glimpsed them after the wagons had circled up. They'd been so thankful for the help she and Owen had provided while they'd been laid up. Maybe they wanted some broth.

She was returning minutes later when Alice darted out of the tent like her skirts were on fire. Just outside the tent lay the spoon.

Rachel sighed. Had she overturned the bowl in her hurry?

When Rachel got close to the tent, a disgusting smell overpowered her. Rachel wrinkled her nose against it.

Sure enough, the bowl was overturned and broth darkened the grass beneath it. But it was the stain on the rumpled blankets that was making such a bad smell.

Alice must not have moved fast enough when she felt herself getting sick. Rachel felt an unwanted beat of compassion for the other woman. Was she in worse shape than she was letting on?

There was nothing for it. The blankets would need to be washed. The tent might need to be moved as well, if the fluid had gone all the way through to the ground.

Rachel would leave that to Owen or the other men.

She gathered up the blankets. There was no one nearby to tell that she was going down to the creek, and she felt a beat of unease at that. A small sliver of soap was all that was left on the tailgate. Hopefully it would be enough. She didn't know where Alice kept her supply and didn't feel right rifling through the other woman's wagon.

She grabbed a torch, for darkness had fallen long ago. It was even darker beneath the trees at the creekbank. Something moved in the brush nearby, and Rachel jumped out of her skin.

A sound of retching met her ears.

"Alice?" she hated the way her voice wobbled.

"Go away," came the thin voice of the other woman from the darkness.

"I've got your bedroll. I'm going to wash it. Are you all right?" Rachel put down the bedding and stuck the torch in the soft ground there at the creek bank. It was flat on this side but the ground rose in a soft muddy cliff of eight feet or so on the other side of the burbling water.

She took a few steps toward where she thought Alice's voice had come from. The torchlight didn't go far, and flickering shadows came from every direction.

Another sound of gasping and retching through the darkness.

"I'm going to get Owen." Rachel said.

"No," Alice groaned. "I'm going back to camp now."

Rachel turned around at the sound of rustling in the undergrowth behind her. She'd thought Alice was ahead and somewhere to the left.

"I can walk back with you," Rachel said.

No answer.

But she'd gone several yards from her torch and now realized that its light was bouncing. Someone had picked it up.

She moved as quickly as her big belly would allow, but it was too late.

She caught sight of Alice's pale face in the flickering light from the torch just before the other woman turned and darted off, taking the torch with her.

Rachel followed, but her skirt snagged on a bramble, and she had to stop. She was too slow. Alice outpaced her, and then the light was gone.

Leaving Rachel in darkness.

Alice had told her outright that she didn't like her. But Rachel hadn't thought she'd do something cruel like this.

Ire piqued, and Rachel thought of leaving the soiled bedroll there on the creekbank. Maybe Alice wouldn't care if she lost it. Rachel didn't even know whether or not she could get it clean.

She didn't want to help Alice. Not anymore, not even if Owen asked her in the kindest, most gentle way. What a mean trick to play.

But there was also a part of her that wanted to prove that what Alice had done had no affect on her.

It was frightening out here. Noises she didn't know sounded around her. A bird call? Or some kind of animal? There was more movement from farther off—another traveler seeking privacy in the woods?

Blood pulsed in the lobes of her ears, and she felt the beat of it where her cheeks met her jaw. She wouldn't let Alice win, the little ungrateful cur.

Rachel scuffed her feet along the ground until her toes tangled in the fabric of the bedroll on the ground. She bent to pick it up, but the baby chose that moment to twist strongly, and something inside her pulsed with pain.

A little off balance, she reached one hand toward the ground in case she fell.

At the same moment, she heard another rustling through the underbrush—much closer than before.

"H-hello?" she whispered.

An animal grunt and more rustling answered.

Fear spiked. A wolf?

Owen had said he'd seen wolf tracks several days ago.

She scrambled for purchase even as something darker than the night streaked a few feet in front of her. Wait—was that a white streak on its back? Could it be a wolverine? She had heard stories of how dangerous they were.

"Help!" But her voice warbled, and who would hear her so far away from camp?

She struggled to her feet. The animal had gone still, but she could sense it out there, nearby. Only a few feet away, maybe.

More rustling and she took off—but her feet tangled in the bedroll. She stumbled, then went to her hands and knees. One arm curved protectively around the baby, but no bite came.

Instead, a terrible smell overcame her.

She shrieked, but the smell got inside her mouth and she gagged.

She ripped her feet away from the bedroll and heard the animal scurrying away through the brush. Her eyes watered so badly at the smell that she couldn't see—not even inky shadows through the darkness.

Water. If she could get to the creek, she could wash out her mouth and nose.

She made it the few feet to the creek bank and splashed her face with water. It didn't help at all. Even the water tasted rancid.

A skunk.

It must've been.

Not a wolf.

She was alive but covered in this awful smell.

Tears ran down her face unchecked. She scrambled back up the bank and rifled through the bedroll for the small bit of soap she'd brought. She couldn't find it in the darkness and the smell was so bad that her throat burned. She had to get away.

Leaving the bedroll behind, she moved through the woods, barely avoiding bumping into one of the trees.

Emerging from the woods meant the starlight helped light her way back to camp. But before she'd even gotten close to the wagon, a dog barked viciously.

She jumped.

How could she walk into camp like this? Alice couldn't have intended for this to happen, but she'd surely rejoice at Rachel's misfortune.

She needed soap. And she had none. No supplies.

But she did have a husband.

Who was busy helping people who needed him. Other families who were ill.

And there was a part of her—a big part—that imagined him laughing the moment he got downwind of her.

He hadn't liked her from the beginning. They'd made an uneasy truce, but he still didn't like her. He might not even help her.

She moved away from the still-barking dog and realized she'd come out of the woods a good distance from Owen's wagon. Alice's too. But as she crossed the prairie grasses, the nearest horses whinnied and shied. Were they scenting her?

The nearest one reared up in the darkness. Rachel took a step back, afraid of thundering hooves.

How was she supposed to pass into camp if she frightened the horses by her smell?

It would be humiliating to ask Owen for help and be refused. Would he send her to the cold creek with no soap?

Her one other dress had ripped. She'd gone to put it on this morning and noticed the big tear down the middle of the skirt. She had nothing else to wear.

Anger surged.

At Evan.

At the trail West.

At her circumstances.

She hated this.

Hot tears fell and she made no move to wipe them away. She was trapped out here in the darkness, alone, unwanted.

Would anyone care if she walked off into the night and never returned?

Six

"WHERE IS RACHEL?"

Owen's demand went unanswered.

Alice was the only one in camp. She wasn't in her tent but sitting hunched over on a crate near the fire looking miserable.

If he wasn't mistaken, a guilty expression flashed over her face before she shrugged.

"You don't know?" he pressed.

A dog barked from a wagon nearby. It sounded like an alert, and the sound put him on edge.

He'd asked Rachel to watch over his sister, to see if she could get Alice to eat something, and Rachel was nowhere to be found.

Some kind of soup simmered on the pot in the fire, and when he strode over to check on Alice he saw a bowl and spoon overturned on the ground outside Alice's tent. He peered inside and found no bedroll. He speared a glance toward Alice. "What happened?"

She shook her head slightly. "She might be down by the creek."

"Why didn't you say that in the first place?" he ground out.

Alice turned green. He shook his head and walked off into the darkness. He was strangely surprised by his disappointment in Rachel. She had done a good job with those kids yesterday. And today she'd walked beside the wagon for a long time without complaining, even though he saw the way she'd put her feet up when they had first made camp and he was unhitching the oxen. He'd thought that things had started to turn between them.

Obviously, he was mistaken.

He passed by horses restless and dancing in the darkness. He had half a mind to go back and get August. His brother hadn't told him about any wolf tracks over the past two days, but everyone had been distracted by the sickness moving through their caravan. Were the beasts out there right now?

Something was out there. He got a whiff of a strong smell that he instantly recognized as skunk and recoiled. But a sound beyond the restless snorts of a horse several paces behind him caught him. Was that someone...crying?

"Who is it? Do you need help?"

The sound instantly silenced, leaving him listening only to the crickets chirping in the distance.

"Rach?" He didn't know what intuition possessed him to call out for her, other than the fact that she'd tried to hide her emotions from him before. His eyes adjusted to the darkness beyond the campfires of the caravan, and he saw a figure standing not far away, a shadow darker than the prairie around it. It had to be Rachel. He strode in that direction and the stench of skunk grew even stronger.

"What happened? Did you get sprayed by a critter?"

If he had thought to make light of the situation, the vitriol in her voice when she answered shocked him into silence.

"I hate you. I hate being out here in the wild. I hate everyone back there." Her voice wobbled, and he had to wonder if her anger was covering something else.

"We can get you a clean dress," he said.

"I don't have another dress." For the first time since he'd known her, she went beyond anger to an edge of hysteria in her voice. He didn't know what had happened to her other dress, but that seemed something that should be fixable. "And it's not just in my dress. It's in my hair. It's everywhere."

He strode the last few feet to her. She must have been right up close to that skunk because the smell was so strong that his eyes began to water. He forced his voice to calm. "All right, so we get you a bath. I'll find you something to wear."

"I don't want to do this anymore."

She had to know she was being irrational. Or maybe she didn't. He'd never seen her break down like this, with great, heaving breaths shaking her shoulders. When he touched her elbow, she turned and pounded her fist into his chest.

"Beat on me if you need to. Punch me if you'd like." It was no less than he deserved after what happened with Daniel. She had a right to be angry with him. She slammed her fist into his chest once, twice, but after only a few seconds, she collapsed into him and sobs shook her thin form.

She hadn't cried when they'd buried Daniel. She hadn't cried when he and August had brought her to the camp after finding her in the wilderness. He wasn't sure what to do with these overwhelming emotions from a normally stoic woman.

She started to pull away, but she was so worked up, her

entire body shuddering and shaking with cries, that he worried for her. He kept his hands on her shoulders and pulled her into him.

"Let's go back to camp and we'll get you cleaned up."

She shook her head, one last shudder shaking her body. "The horses are scared of me."

He hadn't given it much thought after finding her out here in the darkness, but the scent probably *was* scaring the horses.

"Then I'll go fetch some soap and something for you to wear, and we'll go down to the creek."

"The creek is where that nasty beast was," she protested.

"I'll scare him off if he comes back. Taking a bath is the only way you're going to get that smell off you," he reasoned.

She gave in, asking him not to bring a torch.

He hurried through camp, grabbing what they needed. Clothing for her stumped him when he saw the rip in her one other dress. He also grabbed a blanket and a couple bars of lye soap.

She was waiting where he had left her in the darkness, hugging herself with both arms.

He wiped all expression from his face so she wouldn't see any sign of disgust. "August told me about a little pool. It'll be easier for you to get washed off there than in the shallow creek."

She let him lead her away into the night.

And for once, he sorta wished she would grump at him.

* * *

Rachel didn't know where Owen was taking her, and she didn't ask. She felt numb after the outburst of emotion.

She wanted to ask why he had come looking for her, if Alice had said something, or if he'd just decided on his own. But she felt too tired, too emotionally exhausted to even speak.

It seemed like they walked for a long time in the dark, until Owen finally said, "I think we're close now."

She didn't know what he was looking for or how he could even see anything in the darkness, other than vague shapes of trees and the prairie out in front of them.

When they walked under the canopy of the trees, the water sounded different—more a bubbling than a rushing sound.

"I'm not a good swimmer." Her usual fire was doused, her words a simple, quiet statement.

"We're not going to be in dangerous water. This is the pool August found."

She saw him bend over and deposit the bundle that he'd been carrying on the ground. When he straightened up, he reached out his hand to her. "I don't know what it's like under the surface. Hold onto me in case you slip. I don't want you to fall."

She took his hand.

It was different in the quiet of night, with only the two of them out here. His hand felt big and warm as it engulfed hers. He stepped into the water first and gave a gentle tug. He was right—the water had quieted, and this little pool was sheltered by the small saplings on the bank.

"How am I supposed to take a bath with all my clothes on?"

"I'm fairly certain your clothes are doused in that smell too. We may even have to burn them."

She felt only a small beat of disappointment. Her other

dress was ruined—if this one couldn't be saved, then what would she wear?

"How come you can stand the smell?"

"I'm fairly certain that something inside my nose has been burned completely away," he teased gently.

A slightly hysterical bout of laughter clogged her throat. She choked it back, not wanting Owen to realize how deeply upset she was.

She stepped into the water and found the bottom of the pool littered with small stones. The footing was awkward.

"I've got you." Owen slid his arm around her waist. She just felt so drained. Even standing next to him, she felt desperately alone.

He kept his arm around her and gently guided her deeper into the pool. The water lapped at her calves, and then her knees, and then her thighs. And when he finally stopped walking, the water was at her waist. Not quite the same for him, towering above her.

"Can you squat down in the water? If you think it's in your hair, we might as well start washing there." He knelt in the water first, his chest and shoulders still above the surface. When she lost her footing, his hands rested at each side of her bulky waist, steadying her in the water. "I'd rather you hold onto me."

But holding on to his brawny shoulder seemed too intimate. And yet she didn't have a choice, not with the slippery stones beneath her feet.

The water was cool but not cold, and when she asked him about it, he said, "There are some underground hot springs throughout this area, or at least that's what Evangeline's guidebook says."

She knew Evangeline loved to read, having frequently seen the woman with an open book.

"Why are you helping me?"

"Because I'm meant to. I'm your husband."

Something about letting the water come all the way up to her chin evoked the tiniest sense of peace.

"You'll need to take your hair down," he said gruffly.

She had to let go of him to lift one arm. Water streamed from her sleeve, tinkling into the pool. "I'm afraid of losing my pins."

"I can keep them in my pocket." He patted his breast pocket.

She took out one and then another, conscious of his closeness. His warm breath fanned her cheek.

When she placed the pins in his palm, a bead of water rolled off his nose and dripped onto her arm.

"Is the smell fading?" she asked.

"Can't tell. I haven't been able to smell anything since those first couple of moments."

If Evan would've said the same to her, she'd have smacked him playfully. But she was so mixed up in her feelings about Owen. His kindness tonight was unexpected, and she didn't know what to do with it. She went back to unwinding her hair. Hanks of it fell to her shoulder.

She gave Owen another two pins. His eyes glittered down at her. He wasn't smiling.

"It's going to take longer to wash your hair than I thought." She'd never heard his voice so gravel-filled. Something about it made her shiver.

And he felt it. She saw the minute squint at the corners of his eyes, then his arm tightened slightly at her waist.

"It's pretty."

Her hair floated around them now, like strands of seaweed softly tickling. He seemed to shake himself. Cleared his throat. When he spoke again, his voice was cool and even. "I'm sure your husband told you that a-plenty."

For a moment, she felt the beat of loss and grief. But it passed. "Sometimes."

Evan was often focused on his work, taking care of the animals and the fields. Even in the evenings after supper, he'd relax in his chair with a newspaper or book and leave her to clean up in silence.

She wished for more evenings together, but that would never happen now.

"If you lean your head back and wet your hair, I can help you wash it."

She leaned back, but her feet slipped. She wobbled.

Owen steadied her, his arm coming around her more tightly. She felt the muscles in his arm move, the cords of his shoulder against the inside of her arm wrapped around his neck.

"I won't let you float away," he said. "You can trust me."

She hadn't been able to, all this time. Did he know what he was asking?

She tipped her head back again so that the water lapped over her ears and touched her forehead. And jumped when his other hand smoothed the hair back from her forehead. She raised her head from the water, shivering as droplets trickled down her neck.

"I've got the soap here. Hold onto my shoulder so I can use both hands to get a lather going."

There was a prolonged moment where he wasn't touching her, and then his hands came into her hair. He breathed out deeply, a gust of air against her temple. His touch was tentative at first, and then got stronger as his fingers stroked into her hair.

It felt so good. She couldn't remember anyone washing her hair for her in years. Possibly since she was a child and her mother had to help her in the bath.

Her eyes closed as pleasure washed over her, flushing her face with warmth. Tears gathered under her eyelids. She hated it that Owen was the one bringing such a pleasant feeling to her.

For a moment, his beard brushed the sensitive skin of her jaw near her ear. Then the soft touch was gone.

He cleared his throat again, but when he spoke, his voice held a hint of a snap. "If you hate being out here so much, why'd you come? Why not stay in the East?"

This felt safer, a return to the prickliness between them.

"I wasn't given a choice." She hadn't meant it to, but one tear slipped free and dripped down her face and off her chin. Maybe he hadn't noticed in the darkness with water flowing all over the place.

"Did you tell your husband you wanted to stay?"

"Of course I did," she snapped. A hint of fire breathed out with the words. "He was too enraptured by the idea of the golden land out west. My brother had already decided to go, and Evan believed it was for the best."

They'd fought about it, bitterly, the day he'd come home and told her he'd sold the house. Her tears hadn't mattered, her pleas for the safety of the baby.

And now both Evan and Daniel were gone. Glinda and Simon, too.

"He loved me," she said fiercely, because she needed to say it, to believe it.

"I know he must've," Owen breathed.

"It was a bad decision. That's all."

More tears fell now, even after she'd thought she was all cried out.

"Lean your head back," he murmured.

Evan had wanted this life, but she didn't. And Evan was gone.

There was no more fight in her. Tears tracked down her cheeks as Owen gently scrubbed the soap from her hair. His hands formed gentle combs that brushed through the long strands in the water. His other hand came behind her upper back, supporting her body.

It almost felt as if he cared.

And maybe that hurt more than anything else, because she knew it wasn't true.

Seven

THE AWFUL SCENT had burned away Rachel's ability to smell. Owen had washed her hair twice, scrubbing for a longer duration each time. He'd been much more patient than she would've been, and his tender touch had moved her in an unexpected way.

Then he'd left her to undress in the darkness, still in the water, so she could scrub her entire body with lye soap.

She'd done so quickly, afraid of the things she couldn't see in the dark. And then she climbed onto the bank where he'd left a dry blanket for her to wrap herself in.

Sitting wrapped in the blanket nearly from head to toe, she certainly felt clean. But she couldn't help wondering whether she still smelled like skunk.

The crack of a twig nearby made her heart beat frantically. "Owen!" she cried.

His voice returned from the same direction she'd heard the noise. "I'm here. You're safe."

It wasn't true. Nothing was safe out here and she well

knew it. But his gentle tone as he kept talking and moving toward her in the darkness made her breathing ease.

"You dressed yet? We need to get back." He dropped something on the ground next to her. It landed with a wet slapping sound. His clothes, she realized. The moon had come out, and now she could see a little better.

He'd changed from his soaked clothes into dry ones.

"What am I to wear?" she returned with a snap in her voice she couldn't contain.

He squatted next to her. She was thankful for the darkness even though she was completely covered by the blanket. "I know it isn't ideal, but I brought some trousers and one of my shirts. It'll get you through the night. We can worry about a dress in the morning."

She heard the note of exhaustion in his voice. She knew he'd had a late shift on watch the past two nights then spent all day helping travelers who'd grown sick. And now the hour had grown late while he'd been helping her.

He hadn't complained.

Even though she wanted to protest wearing a man's pants and shirt, she swallowed the impulse.

"Can you stay close?" she asked. "I don't like being alone out here in the darkness."

"It's not that dark. There's plenty of stars—"

Had she been thinking a charitable thought about him? Maybe he wasn't tired at all if he wanted to argue.

"Just turn your back," she insisted. "And then we can return to camp."

A thought that filled her with uncertainty. Would Alice find humor in Rachel's calamity?

He huffed a sound of impatience but walked two paces

away and gave her his back. She sat for a moment, waiting to see whether he would remain there or not.

"Get moving, Rach." His grumble of impatience came without a twitch, and she was feeling the exhaustion of going through this ordeal and a long day walking next to the oxen.

She grabbed the shirt from the ground next to her and pulled it over her head as best she could without losing the covering of the blanket.

Maybe she was getting back her sense of smell because the soft fabric of his shirt had the scent of clean soap and a little of Owen himself. It was so big that it draped down to her thighs. Was this his nightshirt? A tie at the neck allowed her to cinch in the top for modesty.

The intimacy of wearing his clothes made her flush. It wasn't improper, because they were married. But it wasn't something done in polite society. Although that didn't matter out here.

She was too tired to think about it more.

She pushed off the ground, grunting a little with the effort of catching her balance after the time in the buoyancy of the water and then resting on the ground.

"You all right?"

"Yes!" she gasped before Owen turned around.

Her head felt stuffed with wool. She'd been tired so early every night in the first days of her pregnancy. This felt the same. As if she'd driven her body to the edge of what it could endure.

She pulled the pants over her legs one by one then stood in her bare feet on the soft, mossy ground. Even with her belly protruding, she had to hold the waist of the pants in her fist to keep them from falling down.

"I'm finished," she said. "Although I'll need a belt or a piece of rope if I'm to wear these for any length of time."

He turned, and she felt his gaze like a touch. No doubt she must look like a bedraggled dog fresh out of the bath.

It's pretty. What had possessed him to give her hair a compliment? And she must be tired if she was allowing it to float through her brain freely.

He stayed silent and began scooping up their wet clothes.

She looked down at the shoes on the bank. She couldn't help the slight groan that escaped.

"What?" Owen asked without looking at her.

"I'll barely be able to stand lacing up my shoes in the morning. After a day like today, my feet are swollen." She sighed. There was nothing for it. She'd gone barefoot on the grassy prairie, but over the past week, they'd begun to traverse a rocky soil with stones sharp enough to cut the bottom of her feet.

Owen put the items he was holding back on the ground and knelt over them. "Leave them off. I'll carry you back."

What?

She realized he was packing their wet things into the blanket.

"You can't carry me." The words left her without conscious thought.

She heard him scoff in the darkness.

"It's not far. Save you the trouble of lacing up the shoes. You'll want your bedroll when we get back to camp anyway."

She did, but part of her felt irritated that he'd assumed.

"Hand them here."

She bristled at his commanding tone. When she didn't make a move to pick the shoes up, he made a sound of annoyance and scooted over to reach them.

He straightened, somehow having turned the blanket into a rucksack tied around one shoulder and across his back at a diagonal.

His hand connected with her forearm, and she instinctively shrank from his touch. They stood silent in the darkness while all she could hear was his uneven breathing.

"I had my arm around you in the water," he said quietly. "This isn't any different."

She couldn't find the words to tell him that it felt different. When they'd been in the water, she'd still been numb from the skunk and the emotional outburst that had followed. But she also didn't want to trek back all the way to camp with bare feet.

She edged closer to him.

He took it as the permission it was and scooped her into his arms as easily as if she was young Ben. His arm around her waist was a band of strength, but as he took the first step, the arm behind her back shifted, and she felt a sensation of falling.

"Don't drop me!" she burst out. But by then he'd regained his hold. "When I said you couldn't carry me, I meant I was too heavy—"

"You aren't too heavy." He was already walking, taking careful steps in the darkness. "But it'd sure help if you'd put your arms around my neck."

It didn't matter what she said now. The stubborn man was out to prove a point.

She slipped her arms around his neck. He grunted his approval. It felt wrong to have someone who wasn't Evan holding her like this. But after all that had happened tonight, she was too tired to protest, or to refuse his help.

She laid her cheek on his shoulder as they passed from

beneath the trees into the open air. Strands of her hair caught in the scruff at his jaw.

Owen was facing their camp. He could probably see the flickering firelight between the circled wagons. She faced into the darkness, back the way they'd come.

Her eyelids drooped, though she meant to stay awake.

It felt... nice. Comforting. To have someone carry her like this. As nice as it had felt when his strong fingers had massaged into her hair.

But she couldn't forget that they didn't like each other.

She hummed a little, agreeing with herself in her sleepy state. Her little noise seemed to galvanize him to speak.

"If you're scared of the dark, why didn't you take a torch? Why were you out washing bedding at night anyway?"

Alice.

If she told Owen about Alice taking the torch and leaving her out in the woods, he'd likely be angry with his sister. And it would serve Alice right. But for some reason, she couldn't say the words that would place the blame where it belonged.

"I just was," she murmured. When had her eyes closed?

His boots crunched over a rocky place in the ground. She was jostled slightly and realized her head had tipped and her forehead was resting against his neck. She could feel every breath he took.

"Almost there," he murmured.

She must be dreaming because his words sounded tender. Not the usual way he spoke to her. But she dropped off to sleep before she could decide whether she was dreaming or not.

* * *

Rachel was fast asleep by the time Owen strode into camp.

Most of the other families were tucked in their bedrolls or tents. Things were quiet.

He caught the twitch of the canvas flap where Alice should be sleeping when he carried Rachel past the fire.

There'd been no time to finish putting together her tent, not with tending to the sick and helping get the wagons circled up tonight. But as he nudged her bedroll open with the toes of his boot and gently lowered her to lie on it, he regretted that he hadn't found another solution. She was swimming in his too-big clothes. Something about seeing her wearing his things tied his insides in a strange knot.

She looked like a little kid playing dress up, but he hadn't quite been able to keep himself from noticing her womanly curves when he'd been holding her beneath the water and carrying her back to camp.

He pulled the makeshift bundle over his head and set it aside to deal with in a minute. He'd thought Rachel might wake up when he laid her down, but her face remained slack with sleep. At least until he started tugging the top layer of bedroll over her. Then her eyes snapped open, a little wild.

"We're in camp," he whispered. "Go back to sleep."

Her gaze flicked up and down his face before her eyes fluttered closed again. He wrapped the blanket around her and she tucked her face into it. Maybe the dying fire felt too bright for her sleepy eyes.

Or was she hiding from him?

Her hair was wild, rioting curls outside the blanket.

She wouldn't thank him for that in the morning.

He'd been stunned by his reaction when she'd let down her hair in the water. It had floated all around them, a blonde cloud so beautiful he almost couldn't bear it.

He knew she was pretty. A body couldn't help but notice it. But her sharp words and independent manner had made him look at her in a different way.

Something had changed tonight. He couldn't say if it was when she'd sobbed against him, completely lost to her emotions, or the vulnerability revealed in her quiet, numb state until they'd gotten in that pool.

Or the silent tears she'd shed over her dead husband.

It was mighty inconvenient realizing that his wife was more than just a burden to bear.

He stood up and walked around the fire. His stomach rumbled in complaint—he'd never gotten to eat.

The silence coming from Alice's tent was too perfect to mean she was sleeping, so he walked over and squatted by the door, even though the canvas flaps were closed.

"Rachel wouldn't tattle, but I know you had something to do with her being out there in the dark. Like it or not, she's a part of my family—our family—now. You'll treat her as such or it'll be me that tans your hide like you were ten all over again."

No sound came from inside. Maybe Alice really was sleeping. She'd been sick earlier, maybe she was out cold.

If he needed to, Owen would talk to her again in the morning.

When Owen straightened, he noticed Collin's quiet approach. Leo's brother had been on first watch and now hunkered down in front of the fire.

Owen could ignore his growling stomach for the night, but he remembered what he'd overheard a couple of mornings ago. He couldn't know when he'd have another opportunity to speak to Collin, so he decided to cut to the chase so he could find his own bedroll.

He sat next to Leo's brother next to the fire. "Stella and her sisters all right?"

Collin didn't look up from where he played with a stick, poking at the coals at the fire's edge. "So far. Both Stella and Maddie are plumb tuckered from waiting on sick folks all day."

Rachel was too. He almost jerked his chin in her direction, almost said the words with that tinge of pride.

Something had changed in the way he saw her now. He didn't know why, not exactly. But being in close quarters with her and the vulnerability in what she'd shared tonight had hit him hard. *I wasn't given a choice.*

He glanced at Collin, for the first time wondering what the man had seen in Stella. Collin had been the one to discover that Stella was disguising herself dressed as a man. He'd been her protector and helped the rest of the wagon train see her in a new light when her true identity had come out.

Now the man looked a little peaked.

"What about you?" Owen asked. "Feeling all right?"

Collin frowned at the fire. "Better than some folks, but my stomach feels like it's been staging a revolt all day."

Owen felt for the man. "You need to rest. I wanted to talk to you, but it can wait."

He started to get up, but Collin knocked over a small log and sent a whirlwind of sparks into the sky. "What about?"

Owen settled back on his rump. "Is your wife still keeping secrets from the company?" He held back a wince as he blurted the words. August would've eased into the conversation gently. Owen had gone in like a buffalo bull.

Collin's expression went carefully blank. "What secret?"

Owen sighed. "Maybe something about that jewel those

hired guns were after?" It was a guess, and a lucky one, if the minuscule flicker in Collin's eyes was truly his tell.

Owen ran a hand down his face. "I don't want there to be anything that puts the family in danger—and that includes more men coming after your wife because of a stolen ruby."

Collin was silent. He tossed his stick into the fire.

"I was too weak to help my pa," Owen said. "But I want to help Leo—and that means helping you, if you need it."

Collin glanced at him from the corner of his eye. "What d'you mean—about your pa?"

Of course Collin would focus on that. Owen hadn't meant to blurt the words. He'd never told a soul. But now the conversation was open and Collin was listening intently for his answer.

He ground his back teeth, jaw jutting out before he could answer. "My pa was real sick there at the end. He was the one who taught me that a man can't be weak. But I was grieving, even though he wasn't gone yet. When I couldn't stand it a moment longer, I went out for a walk. A long one. Trying to clear my head. Trying not to let my old man see my tears."

His voice shook a little and he did what he could to clamp down on his emotions. There was a reason he didn't talk about this.

"When I came back in, the old man had taken his own life." Saying the words now choked him, and he had to stop.

Rachel rolled over heavily. His eyes flicked to her, but her face was relaxed in sleep.

Collin stared into the fire. He must've sensed how much Owen didn't want anyone to see his emotion.

"Only the Good Lord knows how many more days he might've had. Two? Three?" *And I wanted those days with him*. Owen couldn't say the last.

It was a long few moments before he could speak again. He spent them staring at the night sky, littered with stars. In the far distance, a wolf's howl lifted. *Ow-roo.* The sound was as lonely and broken as Owen had felt in those days after his pa had passed.

He cleared his throat. "Don't tell August. He thinks Pa passed naturally."

Collin nodded. "That wasn't your fault," he said. "What happened."

Owen shook his head. "If I'd have been stronger, he wouldn't have had to do it."

Pa had preached about being strong ever since the tragedy that had taken Ma. Owen had tried to live up to Pa's beliefs, but in the end he'd failed. He'd made a vow to himself that he'd never allow weakness to creep in again. That was why he had to be vigilant and get his family to Oregon.

He looked at Collin. The other man met his stare.

"You figure out how to take care of whatever secret is following you," he told Collin. "Or Leo and I will do it for you."

He saw the protest form on Collin's lips, the frown deepen around his eyes. But then Collin's face turned milk white. His nostrils flared, and he scrambled to his feet, one hand clapped over his mouth.

He ran for the edge of the camp beyond the wagons.

And Owen was left to stew in the past.

Eight

RACHEL WOKE SLOWLY, coming to consciousness in snatches as she faded in and out of sleep.

She dreamed she heard Owen's low voice. "*Let her sleep. She needs her rest.*"

Her dream-memory supplied an image of Owen kneeling over her and gently pushing her hair back from her face. Backlit by the fire, his face was shadowed so that she couldn't read his expression—hard or soft?

A dog barked, and she realized she'd drifted off again. This time she came completely awake, blinking in the morning sunlight.

If it was daylight, she'd overslept.

Her nose twitched at the faint scent of that awful musk. Everything came back to her in a rush.

The skunk.

The pungent stench all over her.

Owen.

The baby swirled gently inside her, giving her a chance to

assess the present moment. Most of the scent was gone. She was comfortable, with faint sounds of camp around her.

She shifted, jostling her little one to stillness. It was easier to think about the baby than about her new husband.

Judging from the stretch against the inside of her skin, Rachel knew time was short. There was nowhere else for the baby to grow. Her nose wrinkled as she tried to remember the last time she'd experienced the false labor pains. A couple of days, at least. But she felt all right. The baby was moving inside her. That had to mean something, didn't it?

She gently placed one hand over her stomach, startled when her palm met bare skin.

A glance inside the bedroll revealed she was still wearing Owen's clothes, and his shirt had slipped up, exposing her belly. She'd forgotten, or maybe she'd put those last sleepy, tender moments out of her mind.

A hot flush seared her chest and neck. What was she supposed to do now? She vaguely remembered Owen bringing their clothing back to camp, but surely her dress would need to be washed properly and hung to dry. There'd been no time to do it last night, with the hour so late. What was she to wear in the meantime?

When she peeked outside the bedroll, the first thing she saw was a pale green gingham dress. One she didn't recognize at all. It sat neatly folded only a few inches from her nose.

What—?

She reached one hand out of her bedroll and touched the material with a finger. There was no note, nothing to indicate that this was supposed to be hers. But what else could it mean that it had been placed so near?

She sat up slowly, easing through the constant ache in her lower back.

What—?

Someone had strung twine between the two nearest wagons and hung a blanket over it to form a makeshift barrier. Crates and barrels had been stacked around the place where Rachel had slept, blocking her from the fire but also from the view of anyone else around. Someone had crafted a little haven in the midst of camp.

How was it possible she'd slept through so much activity?

She could only guess that Owen had done this. Who else would know that she'd want privacy? She'd been barely holding on to consciousness last night when he'd carried her into camp; there'd been no one else awake to see her then.

And Owen had protected her from being seen now.

She didn't know how late it was already, didn't want to waste the moments of privacy, so she quickly donned the dress. It must've been made for someone in her same condition, because it fell over her belly even better than the dress she'd sewn herself, though the shoulders were a little too big.

Her shoes were sitting next to the wagon wheel. She desperately didn't want to put them on.

She heard his voice before she'd decided whether or not to put on the shoes.

"...see whether she's awake."

"I'm awake." Who was he talking to?

She drew back the blanket curtain, knowing it would be easier to move than the crates or barrels all so neatly stacked.

Owen approached with little Mabel in his arms. Fergus had Ethel on his hip, and Margaret trailed a couple of steps behind.

Owen's gaze roamed over her. She became instantly aware that her hair spilled down around her shoulders, her curls a crazy mess. She quickly grabbed the entire mass, twisting it and tucking it behind her head as best she could.

"I've still got your hairpins." There was something new in the deepness of his voice, and there in his eyes, too, as he watched her.

Her mind replayed a memory of Owen sitting by the fire talking to Collin. He'd been speaking quietly, and she knew she wasn't meant to have heard his words, but she would never forget the grief and pain she'd seen in his expression.

She'd spent weeks hating him, never knowing that beneath his controlling exterior, there was a man who felt grief like she did.

The knowledge—and everything that had passed between them last night—settled inside her, made her unsure how to proceed this morning.

"Didja make a fort over here?" Fergus asked. He put his little sister down, and she quickly scampered inside Rachel's shelter.

Something in Owen's eyes glittered. "I thought we'd better re-arrange our supplies from the wagon since we're having a rest day."

She knew better. He'd done it to give her a space of her own.

She didn't know how to feel about it.

"We brought ya these!" Margaret held out two leather... shoes?

Rachel reached out for them automatically, then twisted them in her hands to study them. They were unlike any shoe she'd seen before. Flat and made of thin leather tanned to softness. With tiny beads sewn all over the top of each.

"Moccasins," Owen said quietly while the kids exclaimed

over the "fort" and examined every inch of it. "I thought maybe they would protect your feet but give you a break from your other shoes."

Unexpected emotion pressed inside her chest. "Where'd you get them? And the dress?"

"Traded some folks."

He said it so easily. But there was a faint flush high on his cheekbones.

He seemed grateful when the baby babbled in his arms and he could look down into her face. "You're in a good mood today, little one."

"Are their parents...?"

"Better. Up and around. The kids wanted to come visit you." He said this with a wry smile. "Said they missed you." He winked.

She didn't know what to do with this Owen. A man who wasn't arguing—for once. A man who'd delivered gifts. Desperately needed gifts.

She ducked her head. "I should get breakfast going."

She couldn't see beyond the crates to the fire from last night.

"Already made. Why don't you rest easy this morning?"

Who was this man?

Leo strode through Owen's campsite, ignoring everything else around him to glare at Owen, who was doing his best to repair a leather bridle. "Did you tell Alice that you would commit violence to her?"

Owen looked up at Leo's demanding question.

They'd made it to late afternoon without having a fight in camp, which was a miracle in itself when folks were ill, and tired, and frightened.

Leo had been elected as one of the captains, same as Owen, before the journey started. And right now the anger emanating from him made Owen wonder whether the altercation would be in his own campsite.

"It wasn't like that." Owen kept his voice low, though he felt a surge of answering anger rise inside him. He didn't like being accused.

Rachel had gone off to gather wood with the Schaefer girls, and Collin and Stella had been having a murmured conversation at the tailgate of their wagon, a good five yards away. Owen felt an awareness that they were watching as Leo strode the final feet and closed in on him.

"What was it like?" Leo demanded. "What on earth could make you threaten a young woman when she was ill?"

"She was acting like a spoiled child," he said, his voice rising. "And I can see that you encourage it if she ran and tattled to you."

Something ugly twisted inside him. He'd been tired to the bone when he'd said those words to Alice. And that had been on the heels of watching those silent tears spill off of Rachel's face.

"She shouldn't have to come to me," Leo growled. "Because you should've never said any such thing to her."

Collin's boots crunched in the rocky soil as he crossed the space between them.

Owen attempted to douse his rising temper. Collin was a peacemaker. He'd talked his twin down from two fights that Owen had witnessed. Until now, Owen hadn't taken the time to appreciate the skill. Collin could talk some sense into Leo.

Except Collin came to stand beside his brother with feet wide in a fighting stance and arms crossed over his chest. "You been interfering in mine and Stella's business, too. You've got no right."

Was this what Collin and Stella had been whispering about at different times during the day? They'd kept sending furtive glances in Owen's direction, though he'd barely been at the campsite enough to catch them.

"You're keeping secrets—" Owen started.

"I've got no secrets from my brother." Collin and Leo exchanged a loaded glance, and Owen felt as if he'd been doused with a bucket of cold water from the creek.

Was it true? Was Leo in on whatever Collin and Stella were doing with that jewel? Maybe Owen was the one on the outside.

It hurt and that sparked his temper even hotter.

"Alice put a fellow traveler in danger by leaving her out in the dark by the creek."

"A fellow traveler?" Leo looked disgruntled. "You mean Rachel?"

"Rachel's been agitating Alice for days," Collin said.

In this moment, it didn't matter that Owen knew just how Rachel could be. How she could irritate like fire ants crawling into your boot. That didn't give Alice the right to pull a mean trick and put Rachel in danger leaving her in the dark away from the camp.

He thought again of Rachel's silent tears. If that critter out in the dark had been something more dangerous, Rachel could've been seriously hurt.

"I'm sure Alice has done her share of instigating," he said.

Leo shook his head, his mouth open like he was going to say more.

Collin said, "Maybe it would be best for everyone if we put some distance between our wagons for the next few days." It seemed like he was trying to make peace with that statement, but Owen felt a niggle of suspicion. Was he trying to keep his distance from Owen because Owen had figured out about the secret he was keeping?

"How am I supposed to watch over the family if there's distance between us?" He countered with a narrowed-eyed glance at Collin.

"Nobody asked you to watch over us," Leo said. He rolled his shoulders underneath his shirt like he was itching for a fight.

Owen had had his share of scuffles with August when they were younger, and he felt the urgency to respond rising up inside him.

"August and I have taken care of you and yours on this journey. If it wasn't for us you'd already have lost half your cattle."

Leo didn't seem to like the reminder that he'd needed help. "You can't know that."

"And maybe your youngest brother. He can't seem to stay out of trouble—"

Leo swung, his fist connecting with Owen's left cheek before Owen had time to react. His head was thrown to the side, and he had to shift his feet to stay upright.

Anger spiked and for a second he strongly considered going after his brother. Collin's arm banded over Leo's chest and pulled him back a step.

"You stay away from me. And you stay away from Alice." Leo spat the words even as Collin pushed him another two feet backwards. "We are not family. Just because we share a worthless father doesn't make it so."

Shaking, Owen didn't dare turn his back.

But Leo let Collin push him a few more steps back, then whirled on his heel and stalked away. Collin followed him, throwing one last angry look over his shoulder at Owen.

Owen's cheek throbbed. He passed his hand over his mouth, noticed it shaking. He threw both hands down to his sides, and they fisted without his conscious thought. Who had seen that scuffle? He turned a circle only to find that, thankfully, the nearby campsites were deserted. People must be out visiting or hunting.

He wasn't totally alone, though. He caught sight of Rachel peeking around the back corner of the wagon. Of course she'd witnessed his humiliation.

When he huffed out an angry laugh and took a step towards her, she flinched. He remembered the way Daniel had struck her, the evidence a red mark and later fading bruise on her cheek. That thought made him even angrier. He went the other way around the wagon and out into the open.

He didn't go far, standing with his back to the circled wagons, staring out into the night. He fisted his hands on his hips as angry breaths sawed in and out of his chest.

How had this happened? He'd done nothing wrong.

Maybe he should've found a nicer way to ask Alice to stop acting like a spoiled little girl, but he couldn't see any way that he had done wrong with Collin. And Leo and his family wouldn't be here if it wasn't for Owen. How had everything gone so wrong?

A soft footfall on the ground behind him made his shoulders tense.

"You'd better let me doctor your cheek," Rachel whispered.

He turned to find her holding a small pail of water and a washcloth.

He dropped his hands to his side. She must've taken that as permission because she stepped closer, dipped the cloth in the pail, and then gently dabbed at his cheek.

Air hissed between his teeth as he inhaled. The spot on his cheekbone where Leo's fist had connected throbbed even more under her gentle ministration.

There was a soft swish of water as she wet the rag and then pressed it to his cheek again. This time the cool water soothed his burning skin.

"Go ahead and say it." His growl had softened, but there was no way he could take the hard tone out of his voice. "I've heard your opinions of me. You think I shouldn't have spoken to him that way, don't you?"

Her eyes flicked up, and their gazes caught and clashed under the moonlit sky.

She quickly glanced down again to dip the washcloth. She spoke more to his chest than to his face. "Why should I? It seems like you're chastising yourself enough for the both of us."

She wasn't going to blame him?

He gave into her gentle doctoring for another moment. Long enough for his temper to cool and for him to feel humiliated that she'd witnessed the altercation.

He'd never have expected her kindness, or for her to go easy on him. Had things changed so much between them?

Her gaze seemed to focus on his chin. "I can't believe Collin wouldn't stand up for you after you'd shared your heart with him."

He was taken aback. She'd *heard*?

"That was a private conversation," he snapped. He'd

thought she was deeply asleep or he never would've spoken about what no one else knew.

She withdrew, eyes flicking to the ground. But it was too tender a wound for him to apologize now.

"Don't ever bring that up again," he growled. And he strode off into the darkness.

Nine

SOMEWHERE IN THE DISTANCE, a wolf howled as Owen was picketing his horse at twilight, two days after the awful fight with Leo and Collin. Owen was reminded of the night he'd sat next to Collin at the fire, baring his soul. What a fool he'd been.

He made a disparaging noise in his throat. The horse ignored him, already lipping up some grass, but a small voice behind him asked, "What'd you do that for? You coulda scared the horse."

He glanced behind him to find Ben watching. Before these past two days, Owen hadn't had occasion to spend much time with the young girl August and Felicity had taken in. She was leaning on a crutch, her broken leg still in a cast, the toe of it peeking out beneath her skirt.

"He isn't very skittish," Owen said. "We've known each other a long time. Since I was a teenager."

"But why'd you make that noise?" Ben was a curious sort. She asked dozens of questions throughout the day. At least, that's what Owen had discovered over the past forty-eight hours.

"You sounded mad," Ben prompted.

Owen looked past her to the place just inside the circle of wagons where Rachel was pitching her tent. He'd worked on it for two days straight, - and it was finally ready for her to use for the night.

If he wasn't mistaken, Rachel was hiding a smile in her shoulder. Maybe because Ben had gravitated toward him these past days, as though completely unaware of how inappropriate her curious questions were.

Last night, around the campfire, it'd been *You ever delivered a baby before? Cattle don't count.* And *What's your homestead like, back in California? What's your horse's name?* Then *That's a dumb name.*

"I'm not mad," he said now, wishing for a few seconds of respite. Even though he knew it wasn't going to happen.

"You sure? Cause that grunt sounded like my pa when he was thinkin' on whether to switch me or not."

Ben had lost her father not long ago, and it seemed that talking about him in a matter-of-fact manner helped her somehow.

"Do you need switching tonight?" Owen asked, raising his brows at her. "Been bothering Mrs. Lewis's chickens again?"

Ben wrinkled her nose at him. "A'course not."

But she looked a little guilty and suddenly remembered she was supposed to be helping Felicity with something.

Owen sighed and sent one more longing glance to the twilight blue hills beyond the horses.

True to his word, Leo had kept his distance from Owen for the past two days. He'd shunned Owen at the changing of the watch, had sent a message that he didn't need help wrangling the cattle he and his younger brothers were pushing west, and had outright ignored Owen when they'd both approached Hollis at the same time.

Until now, Owen hadn't realized just how much he'd come to lean on his brother in camp. When Mr. Fink had come to him griping about tobacco smoke from a traveler camped next to him, Owen's first reaction had been to go to Leo about the ridiculous complaint.

"Stop worrying," Rachel said quietly as he helped her set the tent pole that would hold the flaps at the opening of her new domicile. She'd been flagging tonight, he'd noticed. Seemed more tired than usual.

"I'm not worrying."

But the look she leveled on him said she didn't believe him.

Even with his head tucked inside the opening of the tent, muffling things outside, he was close enough to hear her sharp intake of breath.

He ducked his head to see under his arm to see her. One hand curled under her stomach, and she'd gone still in a way that might mean she was uncomfortable. Or in pain.

He finished tying off the tent to the pole. "More labor pains?" he asked with his head still inside.

There was a hesitation before she answered. He had scrambled back outside when she said, "They've come and gone today. A little stronger than before."

She exhaled for a long moment before breathing easier. Her hand smoothed over the fabric of the sprigged calico. With her face slightly flushed and the firelight dancing off her skin, she was beautiful. It hit him the same way it had in several unexpected moments over the past days, ever since their nighttime adventure in the creek pool.

He cleared his throat and ducked his head, afraid to be caught staring.

"I found you another dress," he said. One of the other families had been willing to make a deal for a dress with extra fabric in the stomach, from a woman who'd given birth during their first days of the trail. "Though it sure seems like you may not need a dress like that for much longer."

She busied herself pulling her bedroll from the back of the family wagon. "You didn't have to do that."

Yes, he had.

Her torn dress had been in such bad shape that it couldn't be repaired. The other dress still smelled of skunk. She needed more than one piece of clothing.

She didn't offer a thank you, but he was getting used to her manner. When something mattered too much, she grew quiet.

Owen noticed Felicity near the fire, speaking in low tones with Abigail, who'd shared her wagon for the first part of the journey, before August had married Felicity. August came into camp, a bulky package on his shoulder. He nodded to Owen and set it slightly beneath the wagon, between the rear wheels. Out of sight but not hidden completely.

"It's too quiet in camp tonight," August said.

The sickness that had plagued their caravan seemed to have passed, though one or two travelers were still suffering. Today had been a long, arduous day, and the camp did seem more quiet than usual.

"I miss Abigail's singing," August continued.

Abigail shot him a wry smile from beside the fire. "Supper's almost ready."

"Supper can wait." August pulled Owen's guitar out of the wagon.

Owen didn't feel like playing. Not with the conflict still
unsettled between him and Leo and Alice. But Ben started
clapping, excitement lighting her face.

"Maybe one song." He strummed the guitar, wincing at
the out of tune note. He tuned the strings for a few moments
and then nodded to Abigail. "Any requests?"

"Something lively," Rachel murmured. She'd perched on
an overturned crate beside him.

He raised his brows at her and then went into a rendition
of "Sweet Betsy from Pike."

Ben shrieked with delight when August pulled her off the
tailgate and into his arms, twirling her around the fire.

"Careful," Felicity cautioned with a smile.

They caught a few glances from travelers eating supper
nearby, a few smiles at August's silly antics.

In response to Felicity's warning, August nudged Ben
onto his back so that her arms were around his neck and her
good leg around his hip. He danced his way over to Felicity
and tugged her to her feet.

She didn't protest, though she shook her head in a
resigned way.

The song ended, but Owen realized that just the effort of
playing it had somehow lifted his spirits.

"Again!" Ben cried as August twirled Felicity, even though
the music had stopped.

Abigail started singing "Oh, Susanna!", and Owen
joined her on guitar. Whatever had been plaguing the
woman a few moments ago, she was smiling now, her voice
raised in song.

Ben had slipped low on August's back and had a choke-
hold on him now; August paused for a moment to dislodge
her and set her on her feet, grabbing her crutch from where

it'd been left in the wagon. He whispered something to Ben, who giggled. Then she scampered over to Abigail.

Abigail kept singing, but let the little girl draw her up until they were both swaying around the campfire.

Owen looked to Rachel, who was watching with a hint of a smile on her lips. Her moccasined foot was tapping beneath the hem of her dress. He didn't stop playing, but tipped his head to indicate she should get up and join in the silliness with the others.

Her eyes widened slightly as she shook her head. But he saw the way her gaze strayed. She wanted to be over there. He couldn't imagine her having a shy bone in her body. Did she need a direct invitation?

He let Abigail carry the tune as he turned the guitar to hang off his back, letting the leather strap over his shoulder carry its weight. He started singing, and then August joined in too, though he couldn't carry a tune at all.

Owen held out both hands to Rachel, beckoning her up off the crate.

She studied him for a moment. Long enough that he wondered if she was going to reject him completely. But then she slipped her hands into his and allowed him to tug her to her feet.

He grinned. Her lips widened in a responding smile. He led her to the little circle stomping and swaying around the fire. When she'd joined a laughing Ben, he brought his guitar back around into his hands and started playing again. Rachel shook her head with a laugh. Had she ever smiled at him like this before?

It was such a silly thing, their playing and singing and dancing. But he was happy that she'd given in.

His eyes met August's gaze across the fire. His brother's

expression held a knowing look that Owen wanted to wipe from his brother's face. August winked and moved to spin Felicity.

Ben tried to do the same with Rachel. An unexpected laugh emerged from Owen's wife.

This felt like... family. Like home, in a way he hadn't felt in a long time. From a time before Pa had died. Maybe even before Ma had passed.

He'd needed this. He wanted this.

What would it take to always have this?

Rachel couldn't seem to catch her breath as Ben spun her around, holding on to both of Rachel's hands. She couldn't remember whether this was the third song or the fourth. She hadn't meant to come out here, to make a fool of herself, at all. Until Owen had drawn her out.

Owen caught her eye as he strummed even faster, ending the song with a crazy twang from the guitar then putting his hand over the strings to stop the music completely.

His eyes were dancing as they found hers. She felt a swoop low in her stomach.

This wasn't the disgust or anger that normally accompanied her interactions with Owen. It felt both familiar and terrifying. She was grateful when Abigail interrupted.

"That's enough of that. Come and eat before the stew is burnt to ashes."

Another of the phantom pains gripped Rachel's stomach. She tried to stand still in a way where no one would notice, but of course Owen did. He came up beside her and put his hand under her elbow, blocking her from view from the others. "All right?"

She nodded tightly, trying to force breath through lungs that had frozen.

Her false labor pains today had been really irregular. She'd had one midmorning and nothing else until late in the afternoon. They had been stronger than any she had felt before, bordering on the edge of pain.

The panicky feeling that had come over her these past few days threatened to swamp her again. She had dropped a spoon after breakfast and looked down to spot it and realized just how huge her stomach was. There was a baby in there, taking up all the room. Time was ticking down. It wouldn't be long now before the baby would want to be born.

Rachel had avoided thinking about what was coming for so long, but reality came crashing down on her. She didn't know if she could do this on her own.

The labor pain dissipated, and she turned away, afraid that Owen would see too much.

When she started toward Abigail, who was dishing out rabbit stew, Owen nudged her toward the crate where she'd been sitting before. "Let me stow this guitar and I'll bring you some supper."

She should refuse. On principal, if nothing else. She could get her own food. Rachel wasn't an invalid.

But there was also a sense of relief to have a bit of distance from the others, and a moment of privacy to try and catch her breath.

When Owen returned, he had two bowls of stew in hand. Rachel thought he might sit and talk with his brother, but instead, he settled on the ground beside her, one leg outstretched, the other knee bent so he could rest his elbow on it.

They ate in silence, watching as Ben chattered to whomever would listen.

Abigail disappeared with an extra bowl of stew. Rachel guessed she was going to track down the wagonmaster to make sure he ate. There was some connection between those two, but Rachel didn't know what.

The baby shifted, a knee or elbow protruding against her side, just underneath her ribs. She couldn't help the small gasp that escaped her.

Owen looked at her sharply. "Another pain?"

She pretended not to hear the note of concern in his voice.

"No." She was a little breathless with the discomfort of the baby's movement. "The little one must've liked the dancing. He's pushed his knee right here."

She touched her hand on the knobby little protrusion from her belly.

His eyes softened the way they had once before, when he felt the baby kick.

"Do you want to feel?" she blurted.

She hadn't really meant to say the words, but now that they were out, it seemed rude to take them back. Especially when Owen had been open and warm all evening, and had given her so much these past days.

He reached out gingerly and placed the back of his knuckles gently against the side of her stomach. She folded his hand flat against the spot where the baby pressed against her side.

For a moment she froze under the touch. His hand was warm and wide. Tender. But it wasn't supposed to be Owen's hand. It was supposed to be Evan here with her, awed at how their baby was growing.

She tried to picture Evan's expression. When was the last time he had felt the baby kick? He'd been so busy keeping the oxen healthy and taking care of her needs. The harder she tried to picture his face in her mind's eye, the more her brain supplied an overlay of Owen and the inscrutable look he wore often—like when he'd washed her hair in the creek that night.

Owen's brows crunched together in contemplation and he murmured, "That seems like it hurts."

"It isn't the most comfortable thing."

Looking into his face, she noticed the fine lines around his eyes and mouth. She'd seen them deepen over the past two days as Owen had pretended that he wasn't fretting about fighting with Leo and Alice.

The baby thumped against his hand, and then shifted again, so that her stomach was smooth. Owen removed his hand quickly, looking down at his almost empty plate.

"I've got something for you," he said.

Before she could respond, he took his plate to the little pile that was forming near the fire. They would need to be washed later, and it was probably Rachel's job to do it.

Then he detoured to the wagon, where he pulled a bundle from underneath.

It seem to have some weight to it. As he brought it over, she saw it was covered in canvas. He set it on the ground and gently pulled back the cover.

A small wooden cradle.

She set her plate on the ground and reached to touch the smooth side. It was beautiful. Definitely handmade with a special carving on the end.

"I heard you telling Felicity that a crate with a blanket

inside would work, but seems like you'll need something better as the baby grows."

He was kneeling behind the cradle, and when she looked up at him, he again wore one of those inscrutable expressions. Behind the scruff on his jaw, and the shaggy hair in his eyes, she couldn't read him at all.

Suddenly, it was too much. She stood abruptly. He straightened and took a step back to keep from being knocked over.

She left the circle of firelight and ducked out between the two wagons, walking out into the darkness. She didn't know where she was going. For once her fear of being in the wild was overridden by the emotion rioting through her.

Unfortunately, she heard his footsteps following.

"What did I do wrong?" he demanded.

If he'd been silent, or if he'd have asked the question in any other tone, maybe she could have held her emotion in. She whirled to face him. The light from the campfire, barely flickered behind him, lining the edges of him with gold.

"You heard me say that I had a plan, but you decided to fix things. As if my plan for the baby wasn't good enough."

His face was in shadow, but she could imagine the way his eyes flashed. She heard the frown in his voice, "If you don't want the crib, don't use it."

She wanted the crib. That wasn't the point. "I don't need a man—I don't need *you*—to make every decision for me."

"That wasn't what I was doing."

She jerked her chin upward. "Wasn't it? You're just like my father."

She was aware that her emotions were getting the best of her and she wasn't exactly being rational, but she couldn't seem to help it as everything overwhelmed her.

"I was ready to marry Evan at fifteen. I loved him. He loved me. And my father refused to give permission."

She was shaking with the anger of the recent moments with Owen. It was easier to hold onto her anger than to fight against the grief swirling through her.

"Marrying Evan was the best thing I ever did. It got me out of a household where women were treated more like furniture than people. It didn't matter whether I had an idea that would help the household or make things easier for my mother. My father never listened. Evan was the only man I'll ever love. I could've been his wife sooner if my father would have relented. But he had it in his own mind that I shouldn't marry until I was seventeen, and there was nothing I could do about it."

She hadn't meant to tell Owen all of that. Hadn't meant to speak badly of her father, though everything she'd said was true. Her father was a good man, but he had never considered Rachel's thoughts or feelings. Nor Mama's. Mama had stopped trying long ago, only doing whatever she could to keep father happy. Keep the peace.

It was Rachel who had protested his heavy hand.

Owen stood in silence. She didn't know whether he was angry that she wasn't grateful for the gift he'd given her or sorry for her. She'd lost Evan, lost the one man she loved. She didn't want any tender feelings toward Owen. He wasn't a real husband. Wasn't her baby's father.

He took his hat off his head and ran one hand through his hair, expelling a breath that might be frustration or anger.

"I can't bring your husband back," he said quietly. "And if you want me to stop trying to help, you tell me so. I won't offer any more help unless you ask for it." He mashed his hat on his head and strode back to camp.

Gone was the man who had been dancing with Ben around the fire. She recognized the tense set of his shoulders. She'd done that. Her ungratefulness and the hardness of her heart had obviously hurt him.

But nothing could take away the ache inside her.

Ten

THE NEXT MORNING, Owen was hitching the oxen when August rode up on horseback.

He hadn't slept a wink, had stared at the sky from his bedroll, trying to figure out how he'd gone so wrong trying to provide that cradle for Rachel.

She had unmanned him with her silent tears, with the knowledge that she'd lost everything, and he'd let his emotions get too soft toward her. That's what it was. He had forgotten who they were to each other. Two strangers trying to make the best of a bad situation.

"Where's Rachel?" August asked.

Owen grunted. "She went down to wash up with Felicity."

She hadn't looked at him once this morning, and his gut felt a little like it was on fire.

August's horse danced underneath him like it was agitated. Owen looked more sharply at his brother. August definitely had something to say.

Owen finished affixing the singletree and moved past the oxen to face his brother directly. "What's going on?"

"I went a little farther than I intended while scouting this morning."

"Wolves?"

August shook his head. "There's an eastbound wagon train, passing a few miles to the north of us. It's small, twelve wagons. But..."

But it was headed East.

Rachel had been demanding to go back east from the moment they had rescued her and Daniel. It's all she wanted.

He thought of the anger and hurt in her expression last night. Heard her words in his memory. *Evan was the only man I'll ever love.*

He couldn't bring her husband back—nobody could—but she'd also claimed she wanted to get back to her mother.

August considered him and Owen couldn't tell what was going on in his brother's mind.

"You promised to take her home safely, didn't you?" August asked.

Til death do us part.

The vows he'd spoken over a week ago echoed in Owen's memory. He'd gone into this marriage knowing it was a sham. Knowing that he was going to walk away from Rachel at the end of it.

"I promised her I would take her to Oregon." Then help her figure out a way home.

"If you connect with that other wagon train, you'll get her home that much quicker."

But it would mean abandoning Hollis's wagon train. Leaving August and Leo and Alice behind.

"I can't do that. And you know it."

August stared at him. His brother knew the responsibility Owen carried. August felt it, too. Leo and Alice were city folk. Not used to the arduous travel and dangers of the trail.

"We'll be all right without you. It wouldn't be my first choice, but we'll survive."

Maybe they would. But what if they faced another group of bandits? They still had to traverse the dangerous mountains.

If Owen took Rachel back East, it'd be months before he could reunite with his family. Not to mention that Collin and Stella were still keeping secrets. Danger might be following them even now.

He shouldn't be considering it at all. "I'll think about it."

As August rode off, Owen turned on his heel, mind flying in different directions. He needed to break down Rachel's tent and stow it away. Make sure the fire was out and that there was water in their pail for later in the day.

He had promised his family that he'd be here for them on the journey west. That promise had come before his vows to Rachel.

His movements were almost angry as he pulled out the support pole and the canvas of Rachel's tent fluttered to the ground.

Except Leo wasn't talking to him. Neither was Alice.

He rolled up the canvas of Rachel's tent. There would be opportunity to travel back East after winter was over. August would keep the news quiet. They were passing far enough south from the other caravan that no one else on the wagon train would know about it.

Rachel never had to know.

After he stowed the tent in the back of the wagon, he

stood with both hands on the tailgate, staring into the interior of the wagon without really seeing it.

Rachel had been ungrateful and angry last night when he had simply tried to do something nice for her. But a part of him wouldn't easily forget what she'd said about her father. The man had been controlling. And wasn't that what Owen was now contemplating? Keeping this from her, making the decision for her? Thinking he knew best?

Was that the kind of man Owen wanted to be?

If he told her, there was a small chance she might want to stay on with Hollis's company. Joining another wagon train was a risk when they knew nothing about the wagonmaster or the other travelers.

Rachel had been hurt by her father. He'd seen firsthand how Daniel had treated her. He could only guess that Daniel had acted much like her father. And she'd said that her husband had made the decision to come west on the wagon train without taking her wants into consideration.

Did Owen want to be just like them?

He closed his eyes.

No. He didn't.

He had to tell her.

If she wanted to go back East, he was going to have to take her.

* * *

Rachel was dawdling by the creek as Felicity hurried to get Ben to wash up after breakfast. Ben was finally drying off with a towel.

"Go on without me," she said when Felicity glanced over at her.

There had been an awkward tension in the campsite last night after Rachel and Owen had come back. It had been a relief to slip into her tent last night.

This morning she'd felt like an outsider as the little family, August and Felicity and Ben, chatted over breakfast about their plans for the day. Owen had been nowhere to be seen. She couldn't imagine him making friendly conversation with her after how she'd treated him last night.

She hadn't slept well, and she blamed her rough emotions on that. The labor pains had come back at different intervals all night long. They were still far apart. Maybe only one every hour. But they had gotten consistently stronger.

The baby was ready, and Rachel wasn't.

The panic swamping her had grown and grown, until she felt like she couldn't breathe, even when she wasn't in the midst of one of the labor pains.

Something splashed in the creek nearby. Rachel looked up, expecting to see Felicity and Ben, but it was Alice with what looked like a tub of breakfast dishes.

Felicity and Ben were gone. How long had Rachel been lost in her thoughts?

Rachel had noticed how the distance between his family had affected Owen. She'd often watched him riding through camp and seen him glance in Leo's direction and away again. He was hurting.

"Can I talk to you?" she asked tentatively.

Alice kept scrubbing the dish she was holding in the creek, as if she hadn't heard Rachel at all. It reminded Rachel of the many times Daniel had given her the silent treatment.

Those memories made her angry.

She stood up, wobbling on her feet when the baby shifted inside her. She turned toward Alice. "You can pretend like you don't hear me, but I know that you do. Owen cares about you."

Alice stood. The dish she'd been washing fell into the creek with a splash. She ignored it. "Maybe Owen can't see you for what you are, but I do. You are a selfish cow."

The words battered Rachel, but on the heels of Alice's words, another pain came over her, shivering down her spine and then overtaking her belly with a cramping.

Alice's eyes flashed. "You are so wrapped up in what you've lost that you can't see the good around you. Owen deserves someone better than you."

Rachel was still trying to breathe through the pain that settled low in her belly, but Alice didn't wait for her to respond. Alice scooped her dish out of the creek. She put it in the tub and settled the entire thing against her hip, then stomped away until she was out of sight.

The pain left Rachel weak for a moment, so she put her hand against a sapling that was nearby and tried to catch her breath. She *was* ashamed of how she had acted last night. She had been frightened of the tender feelings growing for Owen. Ashamed that she was forgetting Evan. And she had taken out those feelings on Owen. He hadn't deserved that. He deserved a thank you for everything he had given her these past days.

Rachel studied the dappled light filtering through the leaves onto the skin of her hand. She had been focused on the past. Focused on the fact that she was trapped on this wagon train when she didn't want to be here.

Owen had been right too. No one could bring Evan back. And she missed him desperately, with an ache that seemed to overtake her sometimes. But he wasn't coming back. He was dead.

Still, she couldn't let him go. She had to do a better job of trying to remember the little things. Once the baby was here, she would take pains every day to talk about his or her father, so that Evan could be remembered. The life Rachel had thought she would have was gone, and even though it hurt, she had to start something new.

She thought of Owen and the way he'd laughed at Ben's antics last night. The way he seemed to care about the baby. Yet what they had wasn't a real relationship, a real marriage. It was an agreement.

She heard hoof beats and looked up to find Owen approaching the edge of the woods.

She went to meet him. She was frightened about what was coming, for the labor seemed inevitable now. She needed to tell him about the pains.

His jaw was set, and he was unsmiling as he swung down from the horse.

"August came with some news. When he was scouting this morning, he caught sight of an eastbound wagon train."

Her heart leaped, but she searched his face. Surely he didn't mean...?

"I promised I would take you to Oregon but that didn't take into account that we might come across people heading east."

"I want to go, "she said quickly.

"It's a smaller train. Could be more susceptible to bandits or other dangers." A muscle ticked in his jaw.

But it meant she could get back to her mother. Get back to the safety of civilization.

"I want to go," she said again quietly.

The words she had planned to tell him were trapped in her throat. If he knew that the baby was coming, surely he wouldn't let her go. Was it dishonest to keep it from him?

"It's your choice." He didn't seem particularly happy to say the words.

Tears pricked her eyes. She was conscious of what she'd revealed to him last night. He knew about her father's controlling nature, had seen Daniel's awful behavior with his own eyes. And he was giving her this choice.

"We won't have a wagon," he said. "It'll be the two of us on horseback, with your tent. We'll bring a pack horse or two with provisions. And we'll have to rely on hunting game. But it is a shorter journey back the way we've come than to finish the trail."

It was a frightening thought to leave Hollis's caravan. Travel without a wagon, without a load of supplies...

But this was her chance to go back home. She would do anything to make it happen.

"I want to go home."

Eleven

RACHEL RODE HORSEBACK on a sorrel mare a few yards behind Owen's buckskin. They'd left the wagon train as the wagons had pulled out, heading in a perpendicular line.

Owen had been dry-eyed, saying goodbye to August with a firm clasp of his wrist.

Rachel had felt a beat of guilt at separating the brothers who were obviously close.

The sun was high overhead and Rachel used her sleeve to dab at moisture on her brow. The spring weather was pleasant —it was she who was burning up.

Another labor pain took her, starting in her back and then rounding to encompass her entire body, pressure building low in her belly. She forced herself to breathe, not to clench her teeth or cry out. Her horse made a whuffle noise and tossed its head.

She lost focus for a moment, and when the pain eased off, she realized the horse had lagged to one side, not following directly behind Owen any more.

He glanced over his shoulder, his expression inscrutable

again. She suspected he wasn't happy with her now that they'd left the safety of the wagon train, though he hadn't said anything outright. She put a relaxed expression on her own face and he turned forward again.

August had said the eastbound wagon train was several miles to the north. When would they cross paths? She wasn't sure she could keep Owen from noticing her pains much longer. Being in the saddle was making them worse, she suspected.

They could still go away, she told herself. They'd come and gone for a couple of weeks, hadn't they? Maybe this wasn't labor at all.

One of the pack horses shied a little, bobbing its head. The line Owen had used to attach it and the other two horses to his saddle drew tight.

A sudden pain came with such force that Rachel couldn't help crying out. Her horse gave a few high steps. She struggled to hold onto the reins. She bit off the cry and focused on breathing through the pain as Owen twisted in his saddle. He reined in his buckskin and the two pack horses followed.

She tried to force her lips into a smile, though she knew it must look more like a grimace. The pain was already past.

"You all right?"

It was the first thing he had said to her in almost an hour. A panicky anticipation bubble grew in her chest, threatening to pop. Suddenly she couldn't stay on the horse a moment longer.

"I think I'd like to walk for a bit."

She saw his brows come together beneath the brim of his hat, but pretended that she hadn't noticed his concern as she threw one leg over the horse's back.

He was yards away. "Hang on. Let me help——"

She came off the horse, clinging to the saddle horn as she dismounted. It was awkward with her bulging belly. Her legs were stiff from being in the saddle. Or maybe they felt like jelly because of the pains.

Owen quickly dismounted, coming close and taking her horse's reins. "You want a drink of water?"

She shook her head, averting her face from the intensity of his questioning gaze. The queasy feeling in her stomach made it feel impossible for her to eat or drink anything.

He fell into step beside her.

"How much farther do you think the other group is?" she asked.

"I'm hoping to catch them by nightfall."

Nightfall. What if these pains didn't go away? What if the baby was coming?

No. She couldn't think like that. The pains were fading. Worrying about them was only going to make things—

A new pain came over her, and she staggered for a couple of steps.

"Rach?"

She waved off Owen's concern. "Just tripped. I'm fine."

Could he hear the breathless quality to her voice?

The pain moved off quickly enough, and she felt a rush of relief. See? That one hadn't been as bad as the one before.

But ten minutes later the next pain took her, starting at the crown of her head and moving through her body, every muscle clamping down. She cried out through clenched teeth and leaned forward to put her hands on her knees that were spread wide.

Owen was at her side in an instant. "What's wrong?"

"Nothing," she gasped.

This time, the pain seemed to go on and on. Radiating low in her stomach and up through her entire body.

"You're having labor pains."

"No, I'm not." She gasped the words again.

"Then what—"

"It's just false pains again."

It had to be.

The pain finally passed. She slowly straightened, secretly grateful for his arm beneath her elbow. When she dared to look up into his face, she saw lines of tension radiating out from his eyes.

"Those false labor pains didn't have you doubled over." He sounded angry.

"It isn't time. The pains will move off." She sounded as ridiculous as the disbelieving expression he gave her indicated.

"How long have you been suffering? Why didn't you tell me?" He bit out the words.

"I'm fine," she said.

He shook his head as she spoke.

Another pain came, this time tearing a cry from her mouth, almost a scream.

Owen must have dropped the horses' reins because he was standing in front of her, allowing her to hold both of his hands in what had to be a punishing grip.

"I can't be having the baby right now," she said through panting breaths. "I can't have this baby. Not without Evan."

She hadn't realized she was crying until a tear dripped off the end of her nose.

"I don't think this baby is going to wait for you to be ready." There was no trace of anger in his voice now, only a note of tenderness as the labor pain faded. He came closer and slipped his arm around her shoulders. While she was usually irritated with the man for arguing with her, she was grateful for the support. Her legs felt like jelly.

"Being in the saddle was paining you?" he asked.

She nodded.

"We need to find a place. Somewhere sheltered."

The landscape around them was open and rocky and barren.

More tears slipped from her eyes. "We'll need water too."

"Can you endure if I hold you in my lap?"

She didn't know. But the panicky feeling had burst, and emotion swamped her. What if he was right? What if the baby was coming?

She couldn't have a baby out here in this empty plain.

"I can try to ride again."

He tied her horse to the pack animals and boosted himself into the saddle, quickly reaching down for her.

"I'm a little scared of causing you to have another of those pains," he admitted.

She looked into his face. He appeared completely serious. She didn't think Owen got scared about anything.

He firmed his lips. "Give me your wrist."

The labor pain started when he was halfway to hauling her into his arms. She couldn't help crying out as she went rigid. His horse sidestepped, and she felt the flex of Owen's leg against her side as he fought to stay in the saddle. His arms around her never wavered. He pulled her into his lap, a graceless sprawl, and she waited for the pain to pass.

She was crying in earnest as it finally moved off.

"I've got you." His murmur into the hair at her temple reminded her of another time he had held her like this. The wagon train had been caught in a stampede of buffalo, and Owen had rescued her by pulling her into the saddle with him. He'd calmed her then, but the danger she was facing right now was inescapable. She couldn't quite seem to catch her breath. Each one sawed through her chest frantically, and she began to see black spots at the edges of her vision.

He tucked his jaw against the side of her face, his hand coming to rest over the baby, even as he pushed the horse into a fast walk. "I know I'm not Evan, but I'm going to help you. You're not alone. You hear me, Rach?"

His words broke through the worst of the panic. She took one steady breath.

"That's right. Just breathe."

She took in air until her lungs loosened enough for her to say, "I'm frightened."

"I know." He was so close, his voice a deep rumble against her shoulder, where it pressed into his chest. "I'm going to help you. Can you trust me?"

* * *

Owen was worried, though he tried not to let on. Rachel seemed afraid enough for the both of them.

She'd gone quiet between each pain. That worried him more than anything.

The pains had grown closer together, more consistent, as he held her in his arms and rode as fast as he dared—which wasn't very fast at all.

He'd jostled her once, and that seemed to bring on a pain bad enough that she'd cried out. He was trying not to do it again, but it was necessary to adjust his seat on the horse occasionally.

Water.

They needed water, and shelter for the night.

He'd given up on finding the eastbound wagons the moment he'd figured out she was laboring. What mattered now was finding a place they could bed down for the night, making her as comfortable as he could.

Her back tensed. He'd been holding her long enough to know that a pain was coming on. He worked at making his body as loose and relaxed as he could even though he felt as tense as a piece of leather stretched too tight—ready to snap.

He felt her every muscle lock up.

"Breathe, Rach," he said, his chin brushing her temple when he ducked his head slightly.

She was drawing tight, panicky breaths. They weren't helping.

"I can't breathe," she whispered jaggedly. "I think—" pant, pant, "—I'm dying."

"You're not dying," he murmured, pressing his jaw into the crown of her head as he rejected the thought. "I'm right here, and I'm gonna help you."

He just needed a bit of water. A small creek. An isolated spring. A pond that had caught some of the last rainfall. Anything.

August had said the eastbound train had been following alongside a creek, but they should've run into it by now. His sense of direction was too good to have gotten turned around. Maybe the creek had ended?

He'd have given anything to be back in camp with Maddie assisting. He didn't know anything about human childbirth. He'd watched animals when he'd had occasion. A dog they'd had when he was eight had whelped puppies. Cattle.

This was different.

And Rachel was already as prickly as a cactus.

He prayed for mercy. It was going to be up to him to be gentle.

She needed it.

"We're going to stop soon," he said as one labor pain seemed to roll into another. She gritted her teeth and pressed her face into his chest. He thought he felt her sob.

And then she was shaking and crying in earnest, big sobs that she couldn't seem to control.

She arched, another pain coming, breaths shuddering. Her lips had gone pale. She was getting too worked up. He needed her calm.

"Tell me how you met your Evan," he murmured.

His words seemed to cut through her terror-induced hysterics. She was still in pain, though, because she answered through gritted teeth. "I can't—" she panted another two breaths. "You tell me," pant, pant, "why you never married before."

She wanted him to talk? All right.

"There was a girl once," he said. "When I was fifteen. I thought she was the prettiest thing I'd ever seen. Thought we'd end up together. All of it."

He caught a flash ahead and to the right. Sunlight glittering on water? He used the reins to steer his horse in that direction.

Rachel's breathing had eased, and he had the sense that she was listening, though her head lay against his chest so he couldn't see her face.

He hadn't thought about Myrtle in a long time. Years, maybe.

"You know, I don't even remember now what I liked most about her. She was smart. First in our class at school." Kind of like he imagined Rachel was. "There was an event in town. A fair or something. I went with August; she was there. There were folks from out of town, too."

Another pain tensed her body, and he let his gaze roam ahead. Not much farther. He didn't want to speed up his horse and risk hurting her worse than she already was.

She was breathing deeper through the pain, still listening to him.

"There was one kid. New in town. I'd never seen him before. Older than Myrtle and me, seventeen maybe? I knew from the way he was watching her that he was sweet on her. I staked my claim, ate supper next to her at a picnic table."

He shook his head a little. "He came over and challenged me to arm wrestle. I was tall then, but didn't have as much mass. Arrogant."

She snorted a little.

He found himself smiling, just a bit, when he told the rest. "I lost the arm wrestling and then she went off with him with hearts in her eyes. The end."

It wasn't exactly how it had gone. He'd challenged for a rematch. The other boy had laughed.

Owen had been so angry that he'd thrown a punch—and got socked in the gut. The pain had doubled him over.

"Owen, what's gotten into you?" He could still hear Myrtle's disapproving voice. Saw in his memory the look she'd thrown over her shoulder at him. Pitying.

If he'd been stronger, he'd have kept her. The whole course of his life would've been different. He might've had kids by now. He'd been weak then. Lost that chance at happiness.

"There's never..." she lost her breath as another pain tensed her body, "been anyone... else?"

"Naw. No one's seen fit to hogtie me. Until you."

She laughed a little through the pain.

He looked down and caught the edge of the smile on her lips before the grimace returned.

"I've got to angle us down this gully," he said quietly. "Hold onto me if you need to."

He could see the water, a sparkling clear stream at the bottom of a washout. He didn't love the reedy openness in the bottom of the gully, but it was better than nothing.

He leaned back to keep his balance as the horse went down the incline, the pack horses on their tail.

Rachel's hand gripped his forearm where he held the reins. She breathed through another pain.

It couldn't be long now, not with the pains coming so close together. There wasn't time for more scouting. He'd have to find a safer location after the baby was born.

They rounded a bend at the bottom of the gully and found a rocky outcropping that he liked. It meant he wouldn't have to get all muddy to fetch water. The gully wall was enclosed enough that he could start a fire—and there! Not far off was a dead conifer, its branches white with decay. It'd be perfect to get a fire started.

"Here we go," he said gently, trying to mask the urgency he felt. "If I let you down, think you can hang onto the saddle long enough for me to get my boots on the ground?"

She nodded, quiet again.

He wrapped one arm around her back and with the other he gripped one hand while she held onto his forearm. He let her down as gently as he could.

By the time her feet touched the ground, her legs buckled in another labor pain. She gasped and held onto the saddle while he swung free.

When he reached for her, she sank against him.

"Let me make you a pallet. We're gonna move pretty quick." It only took him a moment to unleash the pack from the pinto. Bless August and his packing skills. The blankets were there on top, as if his brother had known they'd be needed.

Owen tucked Rachel's pallet close to the edge of the bluff. She seemed relieved to be off the horse, lying down. Her face was still pale, though her pulse flew at her neck.

"I'm gonna get a fire going. Boil some water."

Now that he was off the horse, panic threatened to grab him by the throat. His mind jumbled with all the things he needed to do.

He forced a calmness, the same one he'd felt when under fire by those bandits weeks ago.

Within a matter of minutes, he had a fire crackling and a big pot of water on to boil. He brought more blankets, towels. They could sort out the baby clothes and diapers later.

Rachel had thrown back her head, her face flushed as she screamed through the next labor pain.

"Take off...my shoes!" she cried out.

He moved to her, the intimacy of slipping the moccasins off her feet making his face flush—but things were about to get a lot more intimate.

"I want to...lie on my side."

He waited for her to shift but then realized she meant for him to help her.

Careful to keep his muddy boots off her blankets, he gently nudged her onto her side, even as another pain gripped her.

When he would've moved away, she grabbed his forearm in an iron grip and tugged almost violently, until he was lying on his side, supporting her weight.

The pain left, and her head lolled onto his shoulder. "I want Evan," she grunted.

"I know." His cheek brushed hers, they were so close. "But you're doing this now. We're gonna meet your little one."

Another pain took her, and he felt its intensity.

"I have... to push!"

"Then push."

He held her through the effort, but when her cry of pain changed to something else, he was there to catch the baby in his hands.

He stared down at the tiny, scrunched face as Rachel worked to regain her breath.

When he looked back up at her, he couldn't keep the tears from his eyes.

"A little girl," he whispered.

Rachel was crying too.

And when he handed her the baby, careful to cradle the tiny head and body, he couldn't help brushing a kiss on top of Rachel's hair.

She glanced at him, joy shining in her expression.

Twelve

RACHEL COULDN'T SEEM to stop crying.

Owen was stooped over the fire boiling more water. He'd already brought warm water for her to give the baby a quick sponge bath, and then he'd brought a blanket to swaddle the little one.

Rachel looked down at the sweet bundle in her arms. She herself hadn't washed up yet, but she couldn't find it in her to care. This was her daughter. Hers and Evan's, finally here to meet the world.

"You figured out a name yet?"

"Molly," she murmured. "After Evan's mother."

"That's pretty."

She was still watching the baby's face, those deep blue eyes wide and staring quietly. She sensed more than saw Owen stand up, still near the fire.

"I'm hungry." The words burst from her. Owen glanced over his shoulder with a grin. "And thirsty," she said, her voice smaller.

"Here." He brought her a dipper of water. "Felicity sent

along some pan biscuits from this morning. I can hunt up a rabbit when you're feeling a little stronger."

He went back to the horses, who were standing idly several yards away, near the bank of the creek. That they were still saddled and mostly packed showed how much urgency Owen must've felt in those last minutes after they'd arrived in this spot.

He brought her two biscuits slathered with butter. Sat them on the blanket within easy reach.

She raised her eyebrow at him. "Butter?"

"Felicity must've traded for some."

Rachel knew a couple of the families along the wagon train had brought a milk cow with them.

The unexpected treat was divine and she tried not to devour the biscuits like a wild animal. She was chewing her last bite when Molly started fussing. Her little face scrunched, and she let out the tiniest of wails.

"Are you hungry too, little one?" She used a corner of one of the blankets Owen had set nearby to cover up with while the baby fed. She brushed her finger over Molly's cheek. How could someone so tiny have captured her heart so completely?

Evan should be here to meet her. He would've cooed over the head of dark hair, the length of her eyelashes, counted each finger and toe.

But Evan wasn't here.

And somehow, the grief had become less pointed in its intensity.

She missed Evan with a deep sadness. She'd tell Molly at every turn what kind of man her father had been. Faithful. Caring. Dependable.

Rachel's gaze was drawn to Owen, who was unloading supplies from the pack horses, making a careful pile of their belongings. He tied off the horses nearby and then began to walk along the creek bank, scanning the ground.

She could still feel the phantom touch where he'd placed a gentle kiss on her head when he'd handed Molly to her for the first time. Strong, bossy Owen had been brought to tears by the miracle of Molly's birth.

He'd been steady. Not frustrating. Even his tone had been mild and gentle the entire time.

She watched him now, the broad line of his shoulders, the scruff at his jaw, the flash of his eyes beneath his hat brim.

Something had changed between them. She couldn't name it. Was a little afraid of it. She and Owen had been at odds from the beginning. She didn't know what it meant for things to change. Or how she felt about it.

When he turned back in her direction, she ducked her head and pretended she'd been looking at Molly the entire time.

He must've found what he was looking for, because he returned to the makeshift campsite with two long sticks. He used a big rock to pound one into the ground near her pallet and then moved to the other side to do the same.

"What are you doing?" she asked, unable to contain her curiosity any longer.

"Improvised clothesline," he said. "I'll hang a blanket here and you'll have some privacy to clean up. The water's not deep enough for you to have a bath."

She couldn't imagine putting her over-sensitized skin into the freezing creek water. What a considerate thing for him to do.

"It'll be dark in another couple hours."

Surprised, she glanced up past the lip of the gully. The sky had taken on the hue of late afternoon. He was right. The sun would be setting soon.

She shivered a little. They hadn't reached the eastbound wagons. Would they have to spend a night out in the open? Alone?

He glanced briefly at her. "We should be all right. I'll tend the fire all night; it'll keep any critters away."

Could he be certain of that?

He finished rigging the line the way he wanted, then he returned to the horses to pull a blanket from one of the packs.

"I'd like to wash out those blankets and move us. Not far," he added. He must've seen her tense. "Just enough so the scent of blood and fluids won't attract any attention from wild animals."

She hadn't thought of that. But Owen had. He was protecting her and Molly, even though she'd separated him from his family and isolated them out here in the wild.

She sat up gingerly, Molly still in her arms as she arranged herself on the padding of the blankets. It only took a few moments to coax a burp from the baby.

When Rachel laid Molly gently on the blanket, the little face scrunched up and another unhappy wail emerged.

She checked the diaper to find it dry. When she picked Molly up, the cries stopped.

Owen adjusted the blanket, standing close enough to see. "She wants to be held."

"Already spoiled?" Rachel murmured.

"As she should be." Owen's words muffled as he ducked out of sight. A moment later, he brought the pot of hot water, a sliver of soap, and a washcloth.

"I can take her," he offered. "If it's all right with you."

Rachel looked up, remembered how good he was with the

Schaefers' baby. But Molly was so much tinier. And yet, she trusted him. Not because he'd asked her to, but she'd seen his actions.

"Thank you." She handed him Molly, caught his intense stare. "For everything."

She didn't know what she would've done if he hadn't been with her. He'd calmed her panic when her rioting thoughts had played out every scenario in the most frightening way. Gotten her to a safe place and helped deliver Molly. Now she watched him cradle Molly in both big hands before he tucked her in the crook of one elbow.

"You all right?" he asked with a quick glance.

"Yes."

He nodded and then walked away, behind the curtain and out of sight. She could hear his boots crunching the gravelly soil near the creek.

She quickly unbuttoned the top of her dress and began to sponge off her skin, the water cool in the waning day.

She heard a sloshing sound and a clank, as if Owen had filled another pot with water.

"You sure are a pretty one, aren't you? Like your mama." His murmur was so soft. Had he meant her to hear it? Or was he just talking nonsense to the baby?

She heard his footsteps approach, but he stopped near the fire. And that was definitely the clank of the pot being lowered into the coals.

"I'll have some more water for you in a minute," he said, this louder and meant for her ears. "And I'm going to scout down the creek just a bit. There might be a decent fishing spot in the bend." His voice faded slightly as he moved off.

She'd been angry with him for a long time. It wasn't right, but somehow she'd shifted her grief and anger at losing Evan onto Owen when he'd pushed her down that first night. Those first days in camp, everything he'd done had seemed opposed to her and Daniel.

But Owen wasn't her enemy.

Somehow he'd become... a friend?

She trusted him to see her safely to this new wagon train. She hadn't asked him to accompany her back East, and she wouldn't. That wasn't their deal. He'd done more than he'd had to.

As she pulled on the new dress, careful of her aching muscles, she heard...singing.

Owen's baritone carried on the breeze. He was singing one of the tunes he'd played just the other night in camp with his brother. But there was a gentle and tender note to Owen's voice. She imagined him gazing down at Molly with a loving look in his eye.

Her stomach twisted, and for one moment, she wished he'd look at her like that.

What—?

She buttoned her dress quickly, then attempted to smooth out the hair that had fallen from its pins in the chaos of giving birth.

That stray thought was simply because of the high emotion of the day. She didn't like Owen like *that*, no matter what they'd been through.

He was helping her.

And that was all.

* * *

"Don't you think you've got enough wood?" Rachel called out.

Owen swung his hatchet again, and it clacked against the trunk of the small dead tree he'd felled. He'd already spent too long chopping down the rest of the tree he'd used to build that first fire, near where Rachel had given birth. It had seemed like providence that there'd been another one here further downstream.

He left the hatchet for the moment and scooped up an armful of twigs and trunk that he'd cut so far. He made a neat little stack a few feet back from the fire crackling merrily and lighting up the night.

"You're really going back to get more?"

He heard the half-exasperated tone in her voice and one side of his mouth pulled in a smile. "Just to get the hatchet. For now."

He had a pretty big stack of wood to burn, but he'd have liked more.

He'd also have liked to get another several miles away from this creek, but he didn't say that as he strode back to the fallen log and picked up the hatchet.

He hadn't told Rachel, but he'd seen wolf scat and several gnawed bones while he'd scouted earlier. He'd gone as far as he could with her wincing in the saddle with nearly every step the horse took.

But she hadn't uttered one complaint. Perhaps she'd have gone farther if he'd insisted, but little Molly had put up a fuss, and Rachel had been flagging. So he'd called for a halt.

He'd started their fire with their backs to a twenty-foot wall in the gully. A funny-shaped tree with one tall spire growing upward and another growing almost parallel to the ground, only a few feet off the ground, made for a good place to dry the blankets Owen had washed out in the creek.

He'd managed to clean most of the blood from the blankets, and they hadn't left much at the first site. Only a towel so blood-soaked it wouldn't rinse clean.

There was no use looking, but Owen's gaze was drawn to the West anyway.

A far-off howl sounded lonely in the distance. Rachel hadn't seemed to have heard it. Instead, she glanced up from the baby she held in the crook of her arm. "I can hear your stomach rumbling from here. Sit down and eat."

She'd eaten two of the fish from the stringer he'd rigged above the fire. Only bones and heads were left in a neat pile near the fire.

She was right about him being hungry, but Owen was too busy to eat.

"I need to set up your tent," he said.

She shook her head. "Not tonight." She glanced past him, out into the darkness. "I don't think I'll sleep a wink either way. Not until we're back with a caravan." She wrinkled her nose. "Besides, I have an inkling that you're going to say we have to leave early in the morning, and it'd be one more thing to pack up."

She was right. They'd be safer traveling with the caravan. And the sooner they caught up to the wagons, the better.

He took two of the remaining three fish from the stringer and sat down, bobbling them from one hand to the other when the heat burned the skin of his fingers.

"Where'd you learn to fish?" she asked, gingerly resettling on the blanket where she was reclining. Still not complaining, though he knew she had to be tender after her ordeal.

"My pa," he said. "You don't know how?"

She shook her head.

"Because you didn't want to learn?" he prompted.

"My father always took Daniel. I wasn't invited." She said

it in a matter-of-fact way, like it didn't matter one way or the other.

"August and I used to fish all the time, with our pa. California trout are the best there is."

He thought about some of those long, lazy summer afternoons when the harvest had been put in and Pa had taken him and August to the fishing hole. About bare feet in the muddy water, a worm wriggling on a hook, fish frying in the pan back home.

August.

In all the action there'd been today, he hadn't had time to consider how his brother was doing back in the caravan. Would he and Felicity and Ben be making music again tonight? Or would it be a quiet night for thinking?

Would August even feel Owen's absence? They'd been together nearly night and day for the past fifteen months, after August had come back from the gold mine he'd staked with a friend.

But now August was wrapped up in Felicity, in the newness of their love.

"You grew up in California?" she asked now, drawing him from his thoughts.

He crunched into a bone and carefully used his fingers to extract it from his mouth.

"Yes'm."

"I didn't know that." She gave him a sleepy look of consideration. She'd said she didn't think she'd be able to sleep, but she looked fit to drift off right there, without being tucked into her bedroll. She'd been through a lot today.

"Was it as wild as I've read it can be?"

He shrugged. "There was a school, but not a lot of kids attended it. We were taught by one of the mothers. There are towns. We didn't live in one. Did a lot of trapping. My pa had a claim he worked."

Pa had hit his lode only months before he passed. He'd never gotten to enjoy the fruits of his labor.

"What about you?" he asked. He wiped his mouth on his sleeve, only catching himself when she frowned slightly. He lowered his arm and wiped his chin with the back of his hand. He'd never paid much attention to manners. But maybe they mattered to Rachel. "I guess I imagined you growing up in finery in the city."

She'd not been shy about saying how much she hated the wilderness, the dark, the wild animals, the weather.

"Not the big city," she said softly. Her eyes had gone far off, like she was lost in her memories. "Just a small town in Indiana. My mother did enjoy fine things. She had a talent for sewing. She could see a picture of a dress in a magazine and recreate it all on her own."

"What'd your pa do for work?"

"He was a farmer when I was young. Worked in a factory later."

"And you got a full education, I guess? Did you have a good teacher?"

Something crossed her expression. An old hurt, maybe?

"She was... fine, I guess. Do you know, I remember—" She stopped and shook her head.

"What?" Now his curiosity was piqued.

"I remember—I was supposed to have the lead role in our Christmas pageant when I was nine. Daniel had wanted the role of Joseph, but the teacher had given it to another boy. I guess Daniel didn't want me to have a leading role when he was assigned to be a shepherd. He..." She trailed off and then cleared her throat. "He burned my costume on the day of the pageant. When it was too late to fix something else. I didn't get to play Mary after all."

She exhaled an audible breath, staring off into the distance. "Do you know, I can't even remember now why he was so angry about it." She seemed to shake off the memory and smiled at him a bit awkwardly. "I suppose you and August had your own share of tiffs."

They'd had plenty of tussles, though August was such an easygoing person that they'd rarely fought. But what she'd described from Daniel seemed pointed. Intentional. Owen was glad the man wasn't around anymore.

How had Rachel's parents let such a thing happen without punishing her brother? It wasn't right. Part of him resented Daniel. And her parents, for not intervening.

Arooo!

The howl came again. Louder this time. Closer.

Rachel looked up, her eyes wide.

Owen tossed his bones into the fire. He tipped his head to indicate the horses picketed several yards away.

"Look at them. They're calm. It's pretty far off." He didn't say that it had come closer. What did he know about the patterns of wild wolves? It could go in a completely different direction.

He indicated the rifle lying near his bedroll on this side of the fire. "I've got plenty of ammunition. And I'll stay on watch, catch a snatch of sleep here or there."

Her brows creased with concern. "What about tomorrow? Won't you be tired?"

"I'll live." He'd do what he needed to see her safe.

That was the promise he'd made. And he intended to keep it.

Thirteen

OWEN SAT UP WITH A START. Had he dozed off?

It was completely dark, the moon out of sight and only a handful of stars visible from their camp down in this gully.

The howl came again, much closer this time. Was that what had woken him?

He'd let himself take a catnap not long after Rachel had fallen asleep. She'd been chatty—more so than normal, which he attributed to nerves at being out here on their own—and had fallen asleep mid-sentence.

He smiled thinking about it. He'd never seen her so relaxed. Was she just tired from the baby? Was that why her walls were down?

He shook off thoughts of Rachel. That howl was bugging him. It had been much closer that time. And sounded different. A call?

Soft yips drifted through the night air.

That was more than one wolf. August had estimated five, but there'd only been one unique track. The others were more generic, so there could be more.

Were they tracking Owen and Rachel specifically?

He slipped from his bedroll, the night air chilling his skin. Two logs and a handful of kindling grew the fire to a roaring blaze instead of the sleepy, small flames it had faded to earlier.

He checked his gun. Got up and paced to the horses. They were awake and aware, not sleeping, their ears flicking back and forth. That was a bad sign.

Another howl.

This one was definitely a lot closer. It sounded like it could've been just around the bend in the creek. Two answering yips came from the opposite direction. Upstream. The horses neighed low and shifted their feet. They didn't like it, either.

The hair at the back of his neck stood on end. Were he and Rachel being surrounded?

He moved to the fire, grabbed his rifle and held it by the stock. He strode around the dancing flames to squat next to Rachel. She'd tucked herself around little Molly in her sleep, surrounding the baby with her warmth and presence. He'd tried to give her privacy the two times the baby had woken hungry earlier in the night.

Rachel had only been a mother for a matter of hours, but she was good at it. That much was clear.

He reached out and shook her shoulder as gently as he could. When she came awake with a start, he put his finger over his lips. Her eyes opened, clear and alert.

The wolf howled again, from about the same distance. More yips.

Rachel's eyes went wide with fear. She scrambled to sit up without bumping the baby, pushing a hank of hair out of her eyes.

"They're closer," he whispered. "Doesn't mean that they'll come into our camp, but I'd like to be ready."

He nodded to the baby. "She's the most vulnerable of the three of us. Can you wrap her to your chest? I'd like you to have your arms free."

Why? She mouthed the word, but she didn't argue, just nodded with trembling lips.

"You'll have to help me get her settled against you." He'd done it with the Schaefers' baby, but on himself, not another person. He fumbled with one of the thinner blankets, aware of the horses now circling on their lines. Could they sense the wolves out there? Were they getting closer?

He had to put the rifle down as Rachel tucked Molly close to her chest. The baby squirmed once, her tiny rosebud mouth opening to make a mewling sound. Both he and Rachel held their breath.

Then Molly fell back asleep, tucked into her mom.

He had to put his arms around Rachel to get the thin blanket tucked beneath her armpit and wrapped over her shoulder. He was close enough to feel her breath on his cheek.

"Owen, I—"

When he sat back on his heels, he couldn't read her expression. She shook her head.

There wasn't time to talk, anyway.

"Wait here." He left her with the rifle. He'd unpacked all their supplies earlier. Now he was regretting it. They could've ridden off if the horses had been loaded up. But could a horse outrun a pack of wolves if it was burdened down?

He slipped his revolver into the back of his waistband and went to the stack of wood he'd made. He pulled out three sturdy, long pieces. He didn't have time to make real torches, but he stuck the ends of the sticks in the fire until they caught flame.

He rushed toward the horses, sorry for frightening them more. He put the flaming sticks into the ground, stabbing them in like stakes at intervals around the animals. He'd imagined a fence of fire surrounding them, but this was more like flickering posts. He wasn't sure it was good enough, but the horses had hooves to protect themselves. Rachel and Molly were vulnerable.

More howling, more yips. They sounded excited now. His gut twisted in knots.

He untied his buckskin and quickly threw on her bridle. There wasn't time for a saddle, not if the wolves were closing in.

He kept a tight hold of the mare and walked her over to where Rachel stood, that rifle in her hands. She was shaking.

"We may need to make a run for it," he said, keeping his voice as calm as he could.

He brought the horse between the fire and the cliff wall behind them. Surely the wolves wouldn't dare come close to the blaze. But he couldn't be sure.

"Let me boost you up," he said.

Another howl, and Rachel jumped.

The horse bobbed its head.

He handed her the reins, his hand closing over hers for a moment. "You'll need to have a strong hand. She's jumpy with all the noise. It'll be all right."

Rachel's eyes were wide and afraid. He wanted to be able to hold her and tell her everything would be all fine. He didn't know where the intense urge came from, only that it felt right.

But there was no time. He let her use his thigh for a step

and boosted her onto the horse's back. She winced as the horse shifted beneath her, caught his glance. "I'm fine."

He nodded to the rifle. "Use that if you need to. Just don't aim it at me."

He'd thought to get a small smile, but she was too terrified to react to his humor. "You need it."

"I've got the revolver."

She blinked, her fear evident. He needed her to be able to think straight.

"Rach." He gripped her knee with his free hand. "I won't let anything hurt you. Promise."

She started to shake her head but gasped as her gaze went to something behind him.

She tried to raise the rifle. As Owen whirled, he heard it drop to the ground.

A white and gray wolf slunk through the darkness where the flickering light from the fire tapered off.

It wasn't moving toward them. Not yet. But it stared at them as it moved in an arc. Slowly. Methodically.

Owen squatted, reaching sightlessly behind him for the dropped rifle.

Rachel hissed his name.

Where was it? He couldn't take his eyes off the wolf. He abandoned his search for the rifle and rounded the fire, reaching for wood to make another torch.

His eyes tracked two more shadows moving in the dark beyond the first wolf. Did they want the horses? Or had they smelled the blood and fluid on Rachel and the baby and wanted an easier kill?

The white-gray wolf darted forward, teeth bared and snapping. It happened so quickly that he wasn't prepared.

"Shoot it!" Rachel cried.

He sensed movement behind him and hoped his mare wasn't rearing or bucking. He couldn't afford to look.

The pack horses shied. One of them reared, its hooves flashing toward the wolf.

The picket line snapped, and the horse bolted into the darkness.

Barks and yips followed, and Owen prayed that the horse was faster than anything chasing it.

The white-gray wolf had danced back but now approached again with slow, stalking movements. They weren't safe.

Owen reached down into the fire and flung a piece of burning wood in its direction.

The wolf jumped back.

"Owen!"

He turned. A wolf had circled around in the darkness and had somehow climbed on the wide, low branch of the tree. It was within a few yards of Rachel, stalking straight toward her.

He reached behind him for the revolver as he ran toward the danger. He drew the gun but didn't have it aimed—and Rachel was *right there*.

Owen threw himself between Rachel and the wolf just as it pounced. He blocked its open mouth with his forearm. Razor-sharp teeth sank into his flesh. He gripped the fur close to its face, trying to sink his fingers into its eyes or nose— something that would hurt.

Rachel cried out. Had the horse reared?

He attempted to fling the wolf away, but it was heavier than he'd thought. He stumbled, going to one knee. If it got on top of him—

A shriek from Rachel, then she was riding through the

fire, scattering flaming sticks and sending sparks twirling up into the sky.

The wolf yelped and let go of him, an orange glowing coal clinging to the fur of its neck. Owen raised the revolver and shot, the sound loud enough to make his ears ring.

The white-gray wolf ran off into the night, the one that had attacked him following it out into the darkness, yowling the entire way.

The two pack horses left were still agitated, circling on their lines.

Fire was scattered across camp. One corner of his bedroll was flaming. But Rachel's reckless ploy had worked. She'd scared off the wolves.

Molly's plaintive cry rose into the night sky.

* * *

"Stop moving."

"It hurts!"

Rachel ignored Owen's bark and continued dabbing the wound in the fleshy part of his forearm with a cloth soaked in whiskey.

He hissed through his teeth.

"I'm glad it hurts," she said with a snap in her voice she couldn't quite contain. "You scared me, jumping in front of that a-animal—" She tried to contain the emotion boiling over.

It'd been a half hour since the wolves had attacked. Owen had built the fire even bigger. So high that she was overwarm standing so close to it.

The pack horse had trotted back into camp moments ago, and Owen had secured it to its picket.

She'd seen the look of relief he hadn't quite been able to hide. But that's when she'd noticed him examine the blood-soaked sleeve of his left forearm.

He'd put her off as he'd packed up the horses, but she'd insisted they doctor his arm before they rode off into the night. How long until dawn?

She'd been so frightened. That was the reason for her tears. Seeing Owen throw himself toward that wolf had brought on such a punch of fear—

She let the cloth drop to the ground and put both hands on her hips, speaking through the tears falling. She was quiet, though, aware of the baby still nestled against her and secured in the blanket.

"You shouldn't have done that!" she whisper-shouted at him. "What if the wolf had ravaged you—?" A soft sob hiccuped out of her.

"I couldn't let it hurt you. Or Molly." His whispered argument held as much fierceness as the man who'd gone after that wolf.

"You could've gotten yourself killed." She hadn't thought it possible, but he stepped even closer. His injured arm hung at his side, but he raised his other hand to cup her cheek. His thumb gently rubbed her tears away.

"I couldn't bear it if anything happened to you," he breathed.

She drew in breath to continue arguing, but he dipped his head and silenced her with a kiss.

It was the lightest touch, a brush of his lips against hers. He edged back so that the smallest breath was between them. His eyes searched her face.

Her rioting emotions got the better of her, and she stretched up on tiptoe to kiss him again.

This time, his lips closed over hers in a kiss both tender and fierce. The contradiction was just like the man. It shouldn't work, but it did.

His hand slipped behind her head and cupped the nape of her neck. Her fingers fisted in the material of his shirt. She wanted him closer. She didn't want to want him—

With a gasp, she broke off the kiss and took a step back.

What had she done?

"I'm not—I can't." Was that her voice? That wobbling, frightened thing?

She hadn't kissed anyone since Evan. Not even when she'd married Owen. Until this moment, she hadn't had the desire.

She'd betrayed her husband, Molly's father.

She was awful.

Owen watched her, his assessing gaze seeing too much. "All right," he said gently. "All right. That was a frightening thing we went through. Our emotions got the better of us."

He was trying to smooth things over. For her.

He passed his hand over his mouth, turned his face away for a moment. When he looked back at her, there was a distance in his expression that made her want to weep.

She didn't know what she wanted.

"Think you can patch me up?" he asked. "I've got some catgut in my pack. A coupla stitches ought to do it."

She pulled a face.

"It's still early, but if we head out now, we'll be closer to catching up to that eastbound caravan. We can take some torches to light our way."

It was maybe the only thing he could've said to calm her enough to stitch up his wound.

With her head bent over his arm, the flickering light illuminating the jagged cuts he'd sustained protecting her and Molly, and her throat clogged with tears all over again.

She dropped her hands, the needle clutched in her right hand. "Evan tried to protect me," she whispered.

And he'd died.

She saw the realization in the softening of his expression.

"I didn't die," he said quietly. "You're not alone."

She took a breath and tried raising the needle again. He was right. If they wanted to go on, she had to do this.

"I didn't even realize what I was doing," he said idly while she pricked the needle into his skin. He only winced slightly.

"I'm not sure that makes it any better," she muttered.

"My ma died because I didn't take action." He said the words a little breathlessly, like they had to be pushed out of his lungs, past his lips.

The needle stopped for a moment before she made herself go on. She didn't want him to quit talking.

"I was eleven. August must've been nine. My pa was real sick. Some kind of fever. He never got sick, but this time he couldn't get out of bed. It was snowing out, a real blizzard. And Ma went into labor."

Oh no.

"She was afraid of having the baby by herself. August and I were pretty young—hard to be of help when we didn't know what to do. She begged and begged me to take her to our neighbor, a woman who had three babies of her own."

She kept the needle as steady as she could. In her mind's eye she could see Owen at that age. He'd have been confident, helpful. But still a boy. A frightened boy.

"She didn't make it?" Maybe she shouldn't have asked. This couldn't be easy for him to talk about.

"I refused to take her so August took her out in the sleigh —there was an accident."

His broken breath told her all there was to know.

"If she was as stubborn as you, she'd have found a way to get in that sleigh by herself," she said quietly. "It wasn't your fault."

He shook he head. "I should've been stronger. Insisted she stay at home. She was weak—having pains."

His mother had been the adult. Had made her own decision, out of fear. The best decision she could make in the circumstance. Rachel carefully tied off the knot in the thread, trying not to pull his skin.

"I can bandage it myself," he said quietly. Maybe he wanted distance after sharing his past. "I don't talk about what happened back then."

Why had he said that? Did he want her to promise not to tell anyone else? Who would she tell?

"But I thought you should know. I had to get between you and that wolf. My conscience wouldn't stand for it otherwise. I'm not the kid I was back then."

He was a strong, able man. But that didn't mean he couldn't be killed. Evan had been strong. Maybe not as much as Owen, but he'd been capable. A marksman. A hard worker.

And it hadn't saved him in the end.

A further reminder that she couldn't open her heart to Owen. She couldn't bear to lose someone she cared about. Not again.

It was better this way. Not letting her heart get more involved.

But when his enigmatic gaze followed her across the campsite to stow the needle and thread, she felt the tug of wanting to open her heart to Owen.

Stubborn, reckless Owen.

Who'd held Molly so tenderly and sang to her.

A man of contradictions.

A man of honor.

If things had been different...

But they weren't.

She forced herself to turn her face away.

Fourteen

RACHEL LEANED FORWARD in the saddle as her horse climbed the last few paces to reach flat ground as they came out of the gully. Relief flowed through her.

Owen was behind her, still climbing with the pack horses tied to his saddle. He held a torch in one hand. They'd used it to light their way in the darkness inside the gully.

On higher ground, the sky was a blanket of stars. The first edges of the sun were peeking over the horizon in the east. Morning had come.

She glanced west, where the dusky dark blue remained. The direction that August, Felicity, and the rest of the wagon train had gone.

She and Owen were here, somewhere in the middle.

Molly was bundled to her chest. She'd been nuzzling Rachel's throat as they'd made the climb out of that gully. What had been soft mewling cries turned into a gusty wail.

Owen's horse climbed onto the plain. The other two horses were just behind.

Rachel patted Molly's bum to see if she could get her to

ease back into sleep. But the little one insisted she be fed. And now.

Rachel sighed and began unwrapping Molly. She sent an apologetic glance toward Owen. "I'm sorry. Maybe I can feed her while we ride."

"We'll make up the time," he assured her. "Do you want to get down?"

Now it was Rachel's turn to shake her head. Owen had rigged her saddle with extra quilts that he'd carefully balanced so she'd have as much cushion as possible. It had taken extra care to get into the saddle and anyway, there was no shelter out here in the open.

She settled Molly at her breast and found Owen looking toward the west, where the sky was still darkest. His arm was bandaged and the reminder of what he'd done to fight off the wolves made her heart beat slightly faster.

What was he thinking now? Was he worrying about his family? Thinking about August and Leo and the things that he might be missing while he was here with her?

"Will you go back to your homestead in California?" she asked quietly. "After..." *After they parted ways.*

"I think August and Felicity are going to have the homestead." He was quiet, almost pensive.

"What will you do?"

"I'll probably file for my own homestead somewhere nearby. August and I might not see eye to eye all the time, but I want to be close."

She cupped the top of Molly's head with her hand, marveling at the downy soft baby hair and her daughter's ferocious eating. Molly's eyes had closed, and Rachel's heart swelled with love. She looked back at the western horizon, too, at the twinkling stars where the sky met mountains. "Evan had grand plans."

It was as if whatever grief had loosened inside her last night had finally let go of its merciless grip. This might be the first time she had mentioned Evan with the soft tenderness she felt toward him and not the anger that her grief had left her with. "He wanted to build a house. Had it planned out how he would cut logs. We'd have two bedrooms, he'd said. And he had plans for an adobe stove. He'd read about it once in a newspaper and written it all out in a journal."

Owen continued staring at the horizon, this time with his brows drawn. What was he thinking?

Molly finished eating with a soft sigh, going limp against Rachel. This time when Rachel raised Molly to her shoulder to burp her, the baby spit up all over the front of Rachel's dress.

"Uh oh." Owen was right there, still in his saddle. "Let me take her for a minute."

She handed Molly into his capable hands, unable to help noticing just how strong and warm they were when they brushed against hers. He lifted Molly to his shoulder, patting her back, as Rachel used the bottom corner of her skirt to dab at the wet, sticky place on her shoulder.

She was resigned to dealing with a sickly smell of curdled milk until the next time they could stop and wash laundry. It would be a comfort. She had never thought that being able to wash laundry—one of her most hated chores—was something to look forward to.

Owen was still patting Molly's back, but he dipped his head to check on her. The baby had dozed off against his broad shoulder.

He would make such a good father.

The thought struck Rachel as she finished dabbing at her shoulder. Owen had married *her*. If they went back East, maybe they could have the marriage annulled before he traveled West again.

Yet she couldn't bear the thought of him marrying someone else. And she refused to examine why.

"I can take her back," she said.

"She doesn't weigh a thing. You'll have her strapped to you for the rest of the day. Why don't you let me hold her for this first bit?"

She agreed, thinking he would be in a rush to get the horses moving, but he leveled a serious look on her.

"I can't stop thinking about that kiss."

Her stomach dipped. She didn't want to admit it, but she had thought of the kiss more than once over the past hours.

"We shouldn't—"

"Who says we shouldn't?" he asked. His voice held a defiant note, though he spoke quietly. "We got hitched. We didn't plan for it to last, but there's no reason why we can't change our minds."

Her heart flew into her throat.

"We don't get along," she reminded him.

"Maybe that was true at first, but we aren't fighting so much anymore."

"We argued this morning," she reminded him.

"And we found a way to end the argument."

She hadn't known he could smile a roguish smile or that it would send her heart flying even faster.

She had loved Evan for so long. Since she was fourteen and had glimpsed him from across the room at a church social. What she'd felt for her childhood friend had grown into something her heart couldn't contain.

It had hurt too much when she'd lost Evan. She couldn't open her heart to anyone again.

"Do you genuinely like me?" she asked. "Because I'm not sure I will ever love anyone the way I loved Evan."

Some emotion passed over his expression, and he glanced past her. "I think liking could come in time."

That was a no. She had grown up with a father who saw her as less than. She'd been someone to order around, not someone to listen to. Even Evan had put his desires in front of hers when it counted the most, sending them on this journey.

She couldn't bear to do it all over again. Wasn't it better to be on her own, even though it would be difficult raising her daughter alone?

"We could go back to Hollis's caravan," he said urgently. "I can build you that same house your Evan promised you. Find a pretty little meadow just like he wanted."

She shook her head. "That was Evan's dream, not mine. I want to go back to civilization."

A note rang false in her voice, but he didn't seem to register it. For one moment, she saw the future as he described it stretch out in front of her. A house with four sturdy walls, plenty of food on the table. Owen striding inside at the end of a day of work and sweeping a toddler-aged Molly into his arms.

But what would Rachel be in that picture? Would she be a faded shadow of herself, trying to live a life where her choices were limited by the man controlling everything?

"We best get to it then." His face was expressionless, but a muscle jumped in one cheek.

She hadn't meant to hurt him.

And anyway, he hadn't professed his undying love for her.

The man couldn't even say that he liked her.

They rode in silence, at a pace she would've found punishing if it weren't for the care Owen had put into cushioning her saddle.

When Molly woke again, they stopped. After she fed the baby, Rachel stretched her legs for a bit while Owen held Molly. She might never forget the tenderness in his expression when he looked at the sleeping babe in his arms.

But there was no warmth for Rachel as he boosted her back in to the saddle. His eyes flickered when she shifted gingerly before settling into the seat.

She had made the only decision she could bear, and it seemed he meant to abide by it. She was thankful for that. Thankful for a man who would keep the promise to take her home.

But a small part deep inside of her wondered what it would've been like if she'd chosen the other future—the one with Owen in it.

* * *

Owen caught sight of the dust trail rising up long before the other wagon train came into view.

It was a relief to know he wouldn't be spending another night out in the wild with Rachel. Mostly because he knew she was terrified of it.

She had hardly said a word to him all afternoon. They hadn't stopped for lunch, though he had startled a family of grouse and managed to get the rifle out in time to shoot one. They would at least have some fresh meat for supper. His arm ached where the wolf's teeth had torn into his flesh.

He couldn't believe he'd made such a fool of himself.

Rachel had been so upset when he'd thrown himself in

front of that wolf that his gut had told him that she cared about him. Even after she had rejected him, had told him in no uncertain terms that she couldn't see a life with him, he couldn't stop thinking about that kiss.

She had kissed him back. In those first moments, he had brushed his lips across hers, but she was the one who had initiated the next kiss.

Or maybe he had it all wrong.

He felt as foolish as he had on the day he'd lost that arm wrestling match and Myrtle had never spoken to him again.

When had he started to fall for Rachel?

From the beginning, she had shown a toughness and resilience he hadn't expected. Yet he admired her gentleness when it came to caring for Molly. Her tenacity.

She wasn't the selfish person that he had assumed when he'd met her.

But while his feelings for her had grown, obviously hers for him hadn't changed.

It was going to be a particular kind of torture to make it through the last of this journey together. To spend several weeks with her knowing that he cared deeply about her. Knowing she didn't feel that way about him.

He must've been a little too lost in his thoughts because he startled when a shot rang out. As it echoed off the sky, he went to sharp attention, instantly using his legs to make his mount spring in front of Rachel's horse.

He glanced over his shoulder to find her wide-eyed, one hand protectively over Molly's back.

"Are they shooting at us?" she asked.

He wished he had the field glasses that August used sometimes. From here, he could see the white of the canvas of the wagons. They seemed to be circled up, not moving anymore.

The afternoon sun was waning. In another hour or so it would be dark.

Pain pulsed in his arm, but he shifted the reins to his left hand, so he had his right hand free to reach for his rifle. Hopefully he wouldn't need it.

"I want you to take the pack horses and ride behind that rocky outcropping over there." He pointed to a bluff several hundred yards to the north.

"What are you going to do?" She sounded worried.

"I'm going to see if they'll let me approach."

He fumbled with the tethers for the pack horses and then leaned over to attach them onto the back of her saddle. His arm panged at the movement, but he ignored it.

"We're too far out for a shot to hit from here. If you see me go down, turn tail and ride."

She shook her head, her eyes wide, and frantic. "Owen, I don't want to—"

"I need you to do as I say. "

He thought she would argue more, so he slapped her horse's flank. The animal took a few steps, tugging the pack horses behind it. He watched to make sure she was going in the direction of safety. Then he dug in his pack until he found a white handkerchief. He tied it on the end of his rifle like a little flag.

He raised the white flag over his head and pushed his horse into a slow walk toward the wagon train, praying the entire time.

He braced for another shot to come, but it never did. When he was close enough to see details, like the oxen and horses attached to the wagons and a little boy peeking out from underneath one of the wagons, a voice boomed out, "Stop right there."

Owen halted his horse, looking for the owner of that voice. Several men had come out from the circle of wagons and stood with arms crossed or holding rifles pointed at the ground. It was a show of force that Owen recognized.

"I'd like to speak to your wagon master," Owen called out.

A man with a blonde beard stepped out from behind one of the wagons. He had a revolver on his hip and his right hand rested on it. "That'd be me. State your business."

"My name is Owen Mason. I was traveling with a westbound caravan. We lost a good portion of our supplies to bandits. My wife insisted she couldn't make it to Oregon and that she needed to go home to her mother."

The man spat a stream of tobacco at the ground near his feet. "That your wife you sent scurrying behind those rocks?"

Owen nodded. He didn't love the fact that the man now knew Rachel was out there alone, but it couldn't be helped.

"How do we know you ain't one of those bandits?"

"I'm not a bandit. And neither is my wife. We are hoping to travel with your party. We don't have much by way of supplies, but I'm a decent hunter, and I can bring in game for the entire party."

He didn't mention Hollis or that he'd been one of the captains. He didn't want to give the man any reason to send them away.

"We've got a couple of good hunters. We don't need any other mouths to feed."

"My wife and I ran into a pack of wolves last night," he said. "There are a lot of dangers out here and safety in numbers. We won't be a burden. "

Playing on the man's sense of compassion was a risk. Owen had seen how people reacted to the harsh conditions and difficult, long days of travel. Fear was a powerful motivator.

"I am handy at repairing wagons," he threw out as a last resort. The words left his lips the moment he saw the jagged edge on the corner of one of the nearest wagons, where it had been damaged and left unrepaired. "You won't regret taking us on."

A young boy of fourteen or so came up behind the wagon master. The man turned to have a whispered conversation with him.

Owen didn't like this. Being in a position of weakness. Having to rely on the kindness of others. Going into an unknown situation.

He glanced over his shoulder and caught sight of Rachel peeking out from behind the rocks, still on horseback.

He was doing this for her. But what was he getting himself into?

Fifteen

SOMETHING NIGGLED at the back of Hollis's mind. Something he was supposed to remember. Whatever it was, it slipped away like chaff on a stiff summer's breeze.

He dug his leather-bound journal out of his pocket, quickly loosening the leather strings that bound it. He flipped to the place he'd left a stub of a pencil to mark where he'd left off yesterday—or this morning?—and found that he'd called for a half-day of travel. The notes scrawled in the margins indicated they'd traveled over a hundred and twenty miles in the past few days. Yes, it made sense now why the camp was full of lively chatter in the middle of the afternoon.

He walked by one cowboy lazing in his bedroll, head tipped back beneath his hat.

Wait. A silver flask rested beneath the cowboy's hand, tucked at his side, atop the bedroll. Hollis leaned down and caught a whiff of alcohol and unwashed flesh.

He frowned. He had rules. He couldn't keep folks from imbibing, but he didn't allow drunkenness. It was dangerous for folks to lose control, especially out here in the wild. With no doctor on the wagon train.

In lieu of waking up the cowboy—who no doubt needed to sleep it off—he scribbled a note in his journal to take care of it in the morning.

He dropped his journal to his side and kept walking. Had he intended to sneak off for a bath and a shave?

He couldn't remember now.

"He's forgotten to eat breakfast more days than else lately."

That was his wagon. He recognized it.

The furtive, urgent woman's voice had come from just the other side of his wagon and overshadowed the relief he'd felt at the moment of remembrance.

"Maybe he's been busy. Or eaten elsewhere in camp." The male voice that answered was reasonable and calm.

"He's lost weight," the woman argued. "Can't you see it in his face? He's thinner."

"Maybe."

Hollis had drawn even with the wagon. The voices hadn't grown quieter. They didn't know he was here.

"Hollis is his own man," the man's voice went on. "He can take care of himself."

They were talking about *him*. He had enough experience to know that whatever this was, he couldn't let it go on. He walked around the wagon as her voice said, "But he's not taking care–"

Abigail cut off speaking, her brown eyes going wide as she took in Hollis.

August was there, hands at his sides, standing at ease but watchful.

"Something you want to say to me?" Hollis asked. He'd

learned on his first trip across the plains that it was better to quash any hint of unrest at the first sign. On that long ago trip, he'd nearly been killed because he'd let a disgruntled family spread rumors about him. He'd thought the rest of the travelers would use common sense and see that the family was wrong, but he'd had too much faith in the goodness of others.

Not anymore.

He just hadn't thought it would be Abigail causing trouble.

Her brown eyes flashed at him as she propped her hands on her hips. "There are holes in your memory, and I'd like you to admit it."

"Keep your voice down," he said, affecting a calm belied by the way his heart pounded in his ears.

She did lower her voice, but she also stepped closer, leaning into his space. "You've been moody and tense and anybody can see that you're in pain. Why won't you tell us what's wrong?"

The songbird was riled up.

No, she was worried. It was there in the tremble of her lips, quickly pinched into a frown. Hollis's eyes flicked over Abigail's head to August, whose eyes missed nothing.

"I'm fine," Hollis said evenly.

Abigail opened her mouth to argue, but he kept going. Perhaps he could distract her from this line of thinking. "I'm hunting for Owen. I need to run something by him."

Abigail's eyes flashed, and she put one open hand over her mouth. August frowned deeply, a look Hollis rarely saw from his scout.

"Owen left two days ago," August said in a low, even voice. "He took Rachel to join up with an eastbound caravan."

And you've forgotten. August didn't say it. He didn't have to.

Abigail dropped her hand. "Your memory is gone," she whispered.

Hollis felt the blast from the words, as if she'd shouted them across the camp.

An echo of the anger from the past rang in his ears as he closed that last step that separated him from Abigail and took her arm in his hand. "I remember every inch of this trail."

August had shifted a half step closer. Hollis's gaze flicked to him. August must've been reassured that Hollis didn't intend harm to Abigail because he rocked back on his heels.

"But you can't remember whether or not you ate breakfast today," Abigail whispered fiercely.

"I remember enough." But Hollis wasn't sure that was true anymore. Owen was gone? Owen had been one of his most trusted captains.

He shook her arm a little before he let her go. "If word gets out that I'm not fit to lead, there'll be a riot."

Abigail's expression settled into something mulish. She rubbed her arm where his hand had been.

"He's right," August offered quietly. "Remember how people reacted when Hollis was missing after the storm? The constant fighting and arguing?"

She opened her mouth again, but Hollis couldn't afford for her to resist. This was too important.

"I'm fine," he said again. "I know this terrain. I can lead us to the Willamette Valley. It's only recent moments that seem to slip away."

She didn't look convinced.

"Your brother trusted me to get you safely to Oregon," he reminded her. "That's a promise I don't take lightly."

It was a promise he hadn't wanted to make at all, but he would never tell her that.

Her expression softened slightly. "It would be better if you had help."

"I do. You."

He could tell from the way her brows furrowed that she hadn't understood him. "You're the only one in camp who has figured out that there are holes in my memory. You see things others miss. Keep your ears open and let me know if there's something going on in camp I should know about."

She didn't like it. He saw it in the way her nose wrinkled. But she nodded. "I'll be bringing you breakfast every morning."

"Fine." His head was pounding now. He didn't need her picking up on that, too. "I've got to check on my horse."

But August followed him away from the campfire.

Hollis didn't say anything. August kept quiet.

Then Hollis sighed. He knew August could outlast him.

"What?" he snapped as he drew near his horse, picketed with several others. He turned to face August, wishing the other man would simply disappear.

"That's not all of it," August said quietly.

"Yes it is."

Pain pulsed behind Hollis's left eye, and he strove to keep his face expressionless. The holes in his memory were enough to worry about. The headaches were growing less and less intense.

Except for right now, when it felt as if his head was splitting in two.

August didn't believe him. It was there in his expression.

"I know you haven't wanted the position, but I'd like to bring you on as captain," Hollis said. Without Owen as part of the caravan, they needed someone with a strong sense of leadership to step in. And August knew enough about Hollis's injury to be of help.

"I'll do it," August agreed.

Relief settled. Hollis realized he'd been so worried about keeping his secret he hadn't asked what he should've.

"How's the rest of your family? With Owen gone."

He knew about the tensions between the brothers. At the beginning of this journey, he'd confronted Leo and Owen, who couldn't seem to hold a civil conversation. He'd thought things had improved in that family. But if things were better, why would Owen leave?

August shook his head. "I'm worried the family is falling apart."

* * *

"Put that down."

"That's mine!"

Rachel came to awareness in an instant.

The sunlight was bright where it flooded through the canvas of her tent, and she realized camp was bustling around her.

Camp.

The new wagon train.

Molly was still asleep, swaddled in the blanket just as she'd been after her last feeding in the darkest part of night.

Rachel felt as if she had slept for longer than she should've. But she didn't dare wake up the baby, not when she could take a few moments on her own, for today would be a long traveling day for Molly.

Rachel ran her fingers through her hair and pinned it up in a loose bun behind her head. She slipped her dress over her head, grimacing when she caught a whiff of the old scent of milk still left from yesterday. There was nothing she could do about it now.

She felt discombobulated from another night of broken sleep. And uncertain about what the day would bring. Owen had been quiet and had spent most of last night studying the people around them, trying to get a feel for the travelers they'd joined.

Someone was tussling nearby. She heard the distinct sounds as she slipped out of the canvas flap and into the morning. Owen glanced up from where he squatted near a small fire. He had the coffee pot in one hand and a tin cup in the other.

Beyond him, at the next campfire over, two teenage boys were pushing and shoving.

There were people nearby. A husband and wife packing up a wagon. A man who might be one of the teens' fathers hauling a pail of water. As she watched, he poured it over a smoldering fire.

Everyone seemed to ignore the fighting.

The bigger boy grabbed what looked like a piece of meat from the other teen's hand. He stuffed it in his mouth.

The shorter boy grew red in the face. He shoved the other boy. "You stole my breakfast."

"So? What are you gonna do about it?"

The taller boy smacked the shorter one on the back of the head, then shoved him to his knees in the dirt.

If no one else was going to say anything about this behavior—

Rachel had her mouth open, ready to intervene, but Owen shook his head at her.

She frowned.

The smaller boy slunk over to a woman in a worn dress—his mother?—and whined, "He stole my breakfast."

"Maybe you should've ate it faster." She cuffed him on the ear. "I ain't got no more. Go wash up and get the oxen hitched." The woman sent a furtive glance in Rachel's direction and then glared at her.

Owen motioned Rachel over. She came to sit on a crate next to him. She had never seen a mother speak so unkindly to her child.

Hollis would've never tolerated such uncouth behavior.

"Don't say it," Owen said under his breath as she settled next to him. He pressed the coffee tin into her hand. There was only one cup. He must've made it for himself. She offered it back to him, but he shook his head. There were tired lines around his eyes. Had he gotten any sleep at all?

"The biscuits are just about done frying," he said. He'd only made four. The dough didn't fill the pan. She felt a surprising pang of missing Felicity and Ben.

"Why didn't you wake me?" she asked.

"I'd rather you didn't say anything about Hollis and his caravan. Let's see how things play out." Owen's words from last night echoed in her mind.

He hadn't divulged what had passed between him and the wagon master. She only knew that she'd been terrified as she had watched Owen atop his horse conversing with the people from the wagon train. He'd been an easy target.

There was no missing the suspicious glances they had

received last night as Owen had set up her tent between two of the wagons. She'd been so tired from the long day of riding and still recovering from the ordeal of childbirth that she'd been asleep before the sun had even gone down.

"You needed your rest," he said now. He took the pan out of the coals using a stick.

"I can decide that for myself." She'd barely breathed the words when he sent a quelling look that only served to rile her up more.

Why was he being bossy this morning?

He tipped his head close. To anyone walking by, it would've looked like they were sharing an intimate moment of conversation.

"It'll be helpful if you can try not to make a fuss."

He must've seen the way her nostrils flared.

"I'll try to remember to ask and to give you space." Now his words were barely audible. "There's enough fighting going on around here."

While she and Owen had been talking, the older teen boy had walked over to two younger kids. He grabbed a biscuit out of the smallest child's hands. A nearby mother said something to him, but he darted away between the wagons and out into the field. And the little boy, who couldn't have been more than four years old, burst into tears. "I'm hungry!"

"I ain't got no more food." The disgruntled mother picked up the pot and several dishes and left the circle of wagons too.

Rachel looked at the biscuits Owen had just pulled out of the fire.

"Don't even think about it," he said quietly. "You need to eat to keep up your strength. And we don't have unlimited supplies either."

He pressed the hot biscuit into her hand. She was ravenous. She was eating for two, and he had a point.

She ate the first biscuit before Molly started fussing. She took a minute to get her daughter and change her diaper and back out of the tent.

"We'll need to wash out her diapers soon," she told Owen.

He nodded. "I'll start breaking down the tent."

"I'm Dr. Goodwin. I heard you'd had a bit of a run-in with a wolf."

Rachel looked up to see a dark haired man with a neatly trimmed beard. He held a black bag at his side.

Owen started to wave him off, but she said, "Hello, Doctor. I did the stitching, and I'm sure Owen wouldn't mind if you took a look."

The doctor's eyes twinkled a little bit as Owen tried to put him off.

"You don't want to risk infection," the doctor said.

With a scowl, Owen agreed to have the doctor check him over, allowing the doc to unwind his bandage.

The doctor said something about her stitching, but Rachel was more focused on the movement nearby. It was the little boy who'd had his breakfast stolen. He crawled beneath a wagon, his face dirt-smudged and streaked with tears.

"Some of the oxen are in bad shape," Owen said to the doctor.

She hadn't noticed. She wouldn't know what to look for. But Owen had.

"Donahoe pushes too hard some days," Dr. Goodwin said.

Donahoe. Was that the wagon master?

He wound the bandage back over Owen's arm. "I'd be careful you don't cross him,"

The boy had crawled closer. Had he noticed her pick up the last biscuit from the pan?

She held the food in her hand and reached her arm behind her, the movement out of Owen's sight. She extended the biscuit as far as she could, hoping the child would understand the offering for what it was.

It only took a second before the biscuit was gone. The child scampered away without even a thank you.

That didn't matter to her.

When she looked back over at Owen, who was flexing his arm to test the new bandage, he frowned at her. Surely he hadn't seen.

"Mason!" Someone barked. Doc Goodwin was already gone.

Owen sent her a serious look. "Stay close today. We don't know who to trust."

* * *

"Miss Rachel, can I see the baby?"

Owen glanced over from where he was tying off their supplies to the pack horses and saw Rachel holding court with two young girls. The morning sunlight played across her hair and face. He had to refocus on his task or risk getting caught mooning over her.

The river nearby rushed and roared. It had provided a soothing sound for his sleep last night, though sleep had been a long time coming.

He had seen Rachel slip the little boy some of her biscuit yesterday morning. He suspected she had found other ways to secretly give the children more food. He should be mad that she was disobeying him. But he admired her compassionate heart.

The children had gravitated toward Rachel last night as she'd cooked over the campfire, but they'd quickly run off when Donahoe had walked through camp. As if they didn't want to be seen.

Owen didn't understand the tension in camp. He hadn't had a chance to run into the doc again to ask about it. It wasn't only that the wagon train was run badly compared to Hollis's caravan. It was something more.

Donahoe was loud and issued instructions in a manner that grated on Owen's nerves. And there was no rhyme or reason to the tasks he assigned.

Yesterday Owen had been instructed to repair a wagon but given no tools or help. Donahoe had been quick to complain about Owen's slow progress. Most of the other men kept their faces averted, but one man with dark hair and a neatly trimmed beard had watched with narrowed eyes.

Owen also didn't appreciate the way most of the men treated their animals. Several of the oxen were limping, obviously having problems with their hooves. When he had tried to mention it, Donahoe had shut him down.

Over the past two days, Rachel had been quiet and watchful. He was thankful that her usual impulsiveness seemed to be on hold for now.

Donahoe crossed the open space at the center of the circle of wagons and came to where Owen was saddling up.

"We're going to cross first thing," Donahoe said.

"The water is too rough here," Owen said without thinking through whether he should've blurted out the words.

Donahoe spat a stream of tobacco on the ground. "I didn't ask your permission, did I? We're crossing here. "

"There's a safer crossing ahead." Hollis's train had crossed there almost ten days ago.

"I'm in charge around here."

Hollis would have never said that. He listened to his captains when they expressed concerns, to August when he mentioned dangerous terrain.

Owen swallowed any further argument.

When Donahoe stomped off, Owen finished buckling the pack onto the horse.

Rachel approached, now without the little girls. Her eyes flicked to where Donahoe had been. "What's the matter?"

Owen shook his head. He didn't want to worry her with his concerns about Donahoe. "I want to ride ahead a few hundred yards and cross where the water's calmer."

He helped her into the saddle, made sure Molly was securely wrapped to Rachel's middle. They set off and rode a half mile, where they reached the shallow crossing. Only Owen's boots and the hem of Rachel's skirt got wet.

"Should we ride back and meet them?" she asked.

He didn't want to, but it would look badly on them if they didn't. And he suspected Donahoe would need help.

By the time they reached the train's crossing, two wagons had come out of the water. The men who'd driven them looked pale with fear.

A wagon was stuck several yards out from shore. One of its wheels might be caught on an underwater rock or tree root. Two men on horseback were in the water behind it, attempting to rock it loose.

Another two wagons entered the water. The young father

driving out front looked petrified as the oxen struggled to pull against the raging current.

"They're in trouble," Owen said. "They're too close to each other."

He couldn't see the driver of the second wagon.

Shouts rose from the opposite shore, and Owen watched in horror as a preteen boy toppled out of the rearmost wagon and into the churning water.

Someone screamed. Owen wheeled his horse into a gallop toward the river.

"Owen, no!" Rachel shouted behind him.

But he couldn't stop. The boy would die if he wasn't pulled out of the raging river.

Owen vaulted off the horse and threw himself into the water as the boy came even with him. The water was so cold that the breath in Owen's lungs froze, and his muscles threatened to stiffen up.

He raised his head above the water trying to see the boy. The kid was several yards downstream, flailing one arm above the water. Owen pushed hard, cutting through the current. His boots were heavy, his clothes soaked and trying to pull him down. The water wanted to claim him as a victim.

Owen threw out his hand and connected with some scrap of fabric on the boy's clothes. He gripped hard and made for the bank, knowing he was no match against the strength of the water but gaining a few inches at a time.

As he blinked against the water streaming down into his eyes, a rope splashed into the water just in front of his face. He grabbed it, wrapping it around his wrist as much as possible.

Rachel!

He gripped the boy tighter, the kid's arms coming around

his shoulders as Rachel towed him against the current. She must've tied off the rope to her saddle horn for she was slowly backing her horse away from the water's edge.

Finally Owen's feet hit solid ground. He pulled the boy up onto land. They both went to their knees on the rocky shore as Rachel dismounted from the horse.

"Owen!" she cried as she rushed to his side, her hands pressing against his shoulders.

The kid was bent over, retching water.

"I'm all right," Owen said through gasping breaths.

Now that he was out of the water, he could hear more shouts from downstream.

Several men were running down the bank toward them.

Owen pushed up on unsteady legs.

"You little fool!" Donahoe grabbed the boy by the arm, hauling him to his feet.

"Why are you shouting at him?" Rachel demanded. "He wouldn't have fallen in if you had chosen a better crossing."

Owen closed his hand over her elbow. She fell silent.

"You better get a handle on your wife. She can't talk to me like that." Donahoe moved toward her, but Owen edged in front of Rachel protectively.

Another man was already dragging the boy back toward the wagon train. Owen couldn't seem to catch his breath, and when Rachel opened her mouth to say something again, he shook his head slightly.

Later, he mouthed.

Donahoe stomped off.

"He didn't even say thank you," she muttered.

Owen turned and embraced her. He couldn't help it. And

he was gratified when she sank into his arms, a shudder of relief emanating from her.

They'd gotten out alive, thanks to Rachel's quick thinking. But Owen didn't know if they could stay with this caravan. Not with such a reckless wagon master. Reckless enough to endanger their lives.

Sixteen

OWEN FELT an even stranger tension in camp this morning.

People were moving around though the sun hadn't crested the horizon yet. Someone was whispering, the sound carrying over the early-morning stillness.

He forced his eyes open. It felt as if he'd only closed them a second ago. Every muscle ached. He'd been assigned on watch during the darkest part of night and had come back to his bedroll exhausted.

"Are you all right?" Rachel had whispered through the canvas of her tent. He didn't know if she'd stayed awake, if she'd heard him leave camp to go on watch, or if she'd been up with the baby.

That she'd asked after him let him know she was wary of their circumstances, too.

There were two people in this caravan that he trusted. One was Rachel herself. The other was Doc Goodwin, who held himself separate from the squabbles and did his level best to help patch up human and animal alike.

Owen had thought he'd understood the dynamics in camp the day he and Rachel had joined, but over the past two days he'd realized something else was at play. Donahoe was often in whispered conversations with a dark-haired man Owen hadn't been introduced to. And Donahoe didn't run things fairly in the caravan at all.

Yesterday, the caravan had come across some stragglers of a big buffalo herd. Owen had asked permission to join the hunt, and he'd taken down one of the animals.

He'd spent two hours in the hot sun butchering the buffalo. When he returned to camp covered in blood and dirt, he'd discovered that Donahoe had given Rachel only two small steaks, claiming the rest of the meat for others.

Owen didn't care about the food. He saw the emaciated figures of some of the travelers. He was happy to help provide sustenance for them. It was the principle of the thing. It had been Owen's kill. He should've had some say in how much he and Rachel received and how much was divvied out to others.

The only saving grace in the moment had been that Rachel hadn't uttered a word of argument.

She was much different than the Rachel who'd swept into Hollis's caravan and pleaded—and when that didn't work, argued—for the help she needed and the outcome she wanted. Owen didn't know whether it was because she was frightened or simply determined to get home.

He heard a footfall in the tall prairie grasses nearby and forced his tired muscles to sit up. The bedroll fell away from his upper body, the cool of morning sending goosebumps skittering up his spine. Or maybe it was the sound of his horses shuffling, like something out in the dark had spooked them. He'd taken to tying them closer than before.

It only took a moment for Owen to spring up and out of

the bedroll, stuff his feet into boots. Pick up the rifle that had rested beside him all night.

He nudged some of the white-covered coals that had been last night's campfire, revealing red hot coals beneath. He quickly put some kindling on top. When it caught flame quickly, he added some twigs. Then he stopped moving and breathed evenly, trying to hear.

Everything was still.

Maybe his movements and the added light had scared off whoever or whatever was out there.

Except then he heard the slow crackle of grasses again, like someone was trying to sneak around. To what purpose?

The first rays of silver light were coming up over the eastern horizon, but he didn't need that much light. Careful of the Gillroy family sleeping underneath their wagon, he skirted the conveyance and moved out into the open, eyes searching the darkness.

He made no effort to mask his movements. And he knew right where he'd put the stake tethering the horses. It only took a few seconds to see the hulking figure that made a darker shadow against the landscape.

One of his horses whickered.

Whoever was out there was awful close to Owen's horses.

"Something the matter, friend?" Owen kept his voice pitched low.

The shape in the darkness stopped moving.

The men on night watch rode horseback and skirted well outside the ring of wagons. This couldn't be one of them. What was he trying to pull?

"You and your missus don't need five horses all to yourself." There was a squeak somewhere in the middle of the defiant statement, and Owen suddenly knew he was dealing with Donahoe's teenaged nephew. The same boy who'd stolen food from his neighbor on that first morning and showed no hint of repentance.

"We do need them," Owen said. He took a step closer to both the kid and his animals. "We don't have a wagon to carry our supplies like you do."

"Mebbe you don't need so much supplies." The boy was trying to sound like his uncle. Owen had seen the man threaten and shout down other travelers over the past two days. He couldn't understand why no one stood up against him. Why everyone looked the other direction and kept on.

Owen wasn't one to shrink from a threat.

"Stealing a horse is a hanging offense," he said. He didn't raise his rifle, but he strained his ears, listening for more movement. He heard nothing. Had the boy come up with this idea on his own? Or been put up to it by someone else?

"My uncle ain't gonna let that happen," the kid said. But in the growing light, Owen could see the way his left hand fisted at his side. He wasn't as brave as he was putting on.

"Your uncle ain't the one standing here holding a rifle," Owen said.

He heard movement from inside the camp and glanced that way. Rachel throwing the tent flap back.

"Kindly move away from my horses," Owen said firmly.

The kid spat—just like his uncle—but huffed and moved off.

The tension didn't leave Owen's shoulders. He stood staring out into the shadowy morning. Who'd been whispering to the kid? He was sure there'd been someone else involved. If they were willing to steal his horse outright—as if he wouldn't know who did it, when they were in the same camp day after day—what else might they be willing to do?

And would Rachel be in the line of fire if something else happened?

Rachel was quiet and a little pale as she mixed up a quartet of pan biscuits for their breakfast. There was no more butter. No little enjoyments in their day. No music.

Owen kept his attention half on taking down their little camp and half on the horses.

Tensions continued high in camp overall. A woman shouted at her husband across the way. A kid was crying somewhere, and there was a hushed, "shut up!"

Owen just wanted to roll out, to try and forget what the mostly peaceful mornings in Hollis's company had been like.

Owen was lashing Rachel's tent to one of the pack horses, his back turned to the camp, when he heard her cry out. He whirled, the tent flopping to the ground.

Donahoe stood close to Rachel. She held one hand close to her chest, Molly cradled in her other arm. She'd half turned away from the man in a protective stance.

Beyond her, the little boy she'd been sharing food with scrambled away, his backside on the ground, a weird shuffle without standing up.

"You leave the Kimballs' boy alone," Donahoe demanded angrily.

Owen had started toward them the moment he'd realized something was happening and drew close enough to hear her quiet, defiant reply.

"He was hungry. Why shouldn't I share my food?"

"You got enough food to share with all these folks?" The wagon master threw his arm wide in a gesture that encompassed the entire camp. "No?" Spittle flew as he spoke. "Then you're just as like to start a riot."

Owen edged in front of her, conscious of Molly's soft

cries where Rachel held her, put one arm out when she would've stepped around him.

"She isn't the one who'll cause the mutiny," Owen said loudly. "It's you and your bad leadership."

There was a gasp from somewhere nearby, quickly stifled.

Donahoe's face went scarlet.

"You think fear and intimidation are the best way to get these people across the plains?" Owen demanded. He stepped forward, away from Rachel and in a way that forced Donahoe to take a step back.

Owen spread one arm wide and swung it in an arc toward the east. "No one here deserves to be treated this way. Having your food stolen. Being shouted at. Fearful all the time. I can lead you. Let me take you back East—"

A dark blur came out of nowhere from behind and on his left side. The first punch knocked Owen's head back. The second one landed in his kidney and tore the breath from his chest.

Off balance, his side and stomach hurting so bad he was seeing stars, he couldn't evade the man who kicked Owen's feet out from under him.

"Owen!" Rachel cried.

Owen looked up from the ground to see the mysterious dark-haired man with feet apart and fists clenched.

He roared, pushing himself up off the ground.

But froze when he heard the sound of a gun being cocked.

* * *

Rachel felt completely frozen as she registered the man with the gun drawn on Owen.

Owen, whose rifle was lying here on the ground beside the dying campfire.

The dark-haired man shared a look with Donahoe and then said, "You don't like our rules, you leave."

She'd never heard a voice so cold. *Our rules.*

She'd thought Donahoe was the one leading, but had that been wrong the entire time?

Molly fussed harder. Rachel shook loose from the terror gripping her to rock slightly. Her stomach hurt, a low pulsing pain that had plagued her since the middle of the night.

Should she run to the horses? Surely that gun could be turned on her just as easily.

She couldn't breathe. She felt hot and then cold, shivering in the morning summer sun.

Owen opened his mouth to speak, but the man cut him off. "Ain't no one leaving with you. Anybody that leaves this caravan is as good as dead out here."

She looked around the camp for someone who might help. She'd seen so much misery, people so hungry they devoured what little food they had like animals.

But the haunted gazes were turned down or away. Everyone close pretended they couldn't hear what was happening.

"Now git." There was something deadly in the man's tone.

"Owen," she murmured urgently. The frozen shell around her was cracking, but she didn't know whether to flee or fight. She could reach Owen's rifle, but not before a shot could be fired.

The man waved his gun, as if urging them on.

Owen backed away, not turning until the man had lowered the revolver to his side.

"C'mon," Owen muttered. She saw the wince he tried to hide with every step.

He'd packed almost everything. Only the coffee pot and his rifle were left. He scooped both up and marched toward the horses. She could barely see for the fearful tears blurring her eyes.

Owen boosted her quickly into the saddle. "Ride out that direction." He nodded back toward the west. "I want to get away from their guns."

He smacked the horse's rump, and the animal jumped into a trot before she'd even fully gotten her seat. A glance over her shoulder showed Owen quickly tying off the tent and other supplies and gathering the reins for the pack horses before stepping into the saddle.

He caught up in the space of a few moments. She reined in her horse, circling to face him.

Molly was wailing in earnest now, but Rachel couldn't think. Knew she couldn't settle enough to feed the baby at the very moment.

"Why did you do that?" Rachel cried.

Up close, she could see the red mottling and growing purple high on Owen's cheek where he'd been hit. She felt a beat of worry for him but pushed it aside.

Owen sent a disgusted look over his shoulder. "I can't believe no one else left."

"Why would they?" she cried again. "How can we make it back East on our own?"

She'd had nightmares of the wolves attacking the past two nights. Only in her dreams, the wolves had knocked over Owen and come for Molly.

Both times, Rachel had woken with a start, sweating with tears running down her cheeks.

There was safety in traveling with the caravan, no matter how difficult the circumstances.

"You wanted to stay on with them?" Now he sounded disgusted with her. "He hit you."

"He knocked the biscuit away." But he'd hit her hand, and her knuckles still smarted. Fatigue made it so she couldn't think.

His eyes glittered. Did he know she was bending the truth?

"They were trying to steal our horses." This was said in a flat voice. "This morning, before camp was awake."

What?

"You should've told me," she said. "We could've come up with a plan. Together."

"When?" Now he was losing patience, one hand thrown up to the sky. "You were already in the middle of trouble by the time—"

"Me!"

Molly wailed louder. Rachel tried to lower her voice, but it only shook with the force of her anger and fear. She'd begun to feel safe with Owen.

"I was trying to do a good deed—"

"One that I told you not to do from the beginning—"

"You aren't my trail boss!" she cried out. He made her so angry. If she'd been closer, she'd have tried to punch him herself. She felt powerless, out of control. "I can think for myself. I can think—not make impulsive decisions—"

He laughed loudly, rudely. "Not impulsive? What do you call riding through the fire to attack that wolf? Or aiming a gun at my brother? You're the most impulsive person I've ever met."

"Well, I wish we'd never met."

She spat the words at him, saw when they hit.

His mouth was open as if he'd been ready to speak, but instead he clamped his lips closed.

He glanced to the side, breathing in and out once, deeply. His eyes were narrowed.

She hadn't meant the words, not truly. But how could she take them back?

He sighed, a long silent breath.

Her heart rose in her throat, tears gathering.

They were alone out here—again. What if he decided she was too much trouble? Just left her and rode on?

"You should take care of her," Owen said quietly. "Want me to help you down?"

Molly's wails had grown frantic, and Rachel's milk threatened release. She nudged her horse so she was facing away from him and loosed the buttons to feed the baby. Molly latched on hungrily and Rachel looked down into her dear face, fear and worry falling over her like a blanket. She had to think about Molly. Getting Molly back home safely.

Hoofbeats sounded, and Rachel glanced over her shoulder to see Doc approaching.

Owen shot her a quick, inscrutable look and moved to intercept the man. They were still close enough that Rachel could hear their conversation.

"I wasn't in camp—I was down at the creek washing up—and just now heard about what happened."

She kept her stare on the gray and purple mountains on the horizon. Who had told him? She'd had such a difficult time trying to talk to any of the other women in camp. And perhaps now she could understand why. The two men had cowed them all.

"You injured?"

"No." Owen grunted the word, his voice low. "Humiliated. I didn't see him coming."

The doctor hummed. "Little Clarence Martin is all healed up. I was thinking maybe I'd ride along with the two of you."

She cut a glance to the side, her heart seizing with hope. One more rider wasn't much, but it was more than just the two of them. Another pair of eyes. Another gun. And a doctor to boot.

"At least to Fort Laramie." The nearest fort to the east, and still over a week away.

Owen grunted. "Why? Aren't you loyal to Donahoe and the caravan?"

She sent him a sharp look but he didn't see it. He was staring at the doctor.

"I joined them from Fort Boise when I saw a need. But I'm in agreement with you. Things are getting dangerous under Donahoe's leadership."

"Then I guess we're thankful to have you along."

The doc said, "I have to admit, when you joined up with the wagon train, I wondered if you were the folks that the deputy was looking for."

Molly was finally satisfied, peaceful and full. Rachel buttoned up her dress and raised the baby to her shoulder, nudging the horse with her knee to turn so she could see the doctor. What was he talking about?

Owen's expression was stormy. "What deputy?"

"He rode through our company a half day before you met up with us. Wore a silver badge and had a sketch of a young woman he was looking for. Claimed she was his long lost niece, run away with her sisters."

Owen sent a speaking glance to Rachel, but she didn't know what had him so riled up.

"Did you believe him?"

Doc shrugged. "He seemed kinda rough to be someone looking for a relative. And young to have an adult niece."

"What did the woman in the sketch look like?"

"Pretty. He said her hair was more chestnut. Maybe even red."

The only person with hair that color Rachel had seen out here was Stella. Or one of her sisters.

Owen's frown had grown thunderous. "We've got to go back west."

"What?" she snapped.

"Whoever that was is looking for Hollis's caravan." And Stella, though he hadn't said as much.

"We're days behind him."

Owen's frown grew at her argument. "I could ride faster on my own."

"No." The anger in her voice stopped him cold. "You promised you'd take me back East."

His face was set like granite as he stared at her.

Doc was looking between the two of them.

"This is my family. Leo will be devastated if something happens to Collin. And we both know Collin will do anything to protect his wife."

"It won't matter, will it?" she included Doc in her plea. "You can't catch up. Even if you abandon us out here."

The muscle in his jaw ticked. "We have to go back to them. Going East by ourselves—it doesn't make a lick of sense. We're going West."

"I won't go!"

It was a bluff, and they both knew it. Owen had the power here. She was terrified of being alone. Those nights she'd spent after Evan's death had wrecked her. Her sense of helplessness expanded inside her, overtaking everything else.

"We're going West," Owen said with finality.

The vows she and Owen had spoken weeks ago flashed through her memory. He'd promised to comfort and keep her.

But he hadn't meant it.

Her husband had spoken.

And she had no choice but to follow.

Seventeen

OWEN PULLED himself from his bedroll as dawn winged its way over the horizon.

Doc sat near the small fire, pushing a coffeepot into the hotter coals with a stick.

Nearby, a little creek burbled.

Rachel was asleep in her bedroll on the opposite side of the fire—as far from Owen as she could manage. Molly was tucked in beside her.

She'd been unhappy with him the past two nights when he'd refused to put up her tent, stating that it would take too long to pack away.

They needed every moment.

The urgency drove him, even now. Someone was hunting Stella. And Owen's brothers could well end up in the line of fire.

He wiped one hand over his face and moved to get up. The muscles in his side protested, and he bit back a groan.

Doc glanced up at his jerky movements, but Owen waved him off.

The deep bruises on his side plagued him all day long. But it was when he shifted in his sleep that the movement stole his breath and made him want to moan.

He slipped his boots on and moved around the fire to Rachel's side.

"Let her sleep," Doc said quietly. "The baby was fussy last night. She didn't get much rest."

"Can't afford to lose the daylight," Owen said.

Rachel was already glaring at him when he bent down. Her expression stayed his hand before he touched her shoulder.

"Time to get moving."

She sat up slowly, her hair rumpled with sleep. There was no softness in her expression—no softness for him at all anymore.

She was pale and seemed listless. Same as she'd acted for the past two days. She was angry with him for changing directions again. Real angry. She barely spoke to him, preferring to address Doc for anything she needed.

The other man was an enigma. He seemed somewhere between Owen's age and what Pa would've been this year, if he'd lived. Owen was too focused on returning to Hollis's caravan to make small talk, but Rachel had had some quiet conversations with the man. And Owen had eavesdropped.

Doc was a nomad, traveling across the prairie on horseback all throughout the summer months. He jumped from wagon train to wagon train.

Owen couldn't figure out why.

Most of the folks he helped surely couldn't pay him.

But Owen could admit that it was a great benefit to have another man along. Doc watched half the night, Owen the other. At least he was getting some sleep.

When he could sleep. He kept having nightmares of gunshots and blood spilled.

"Best hurry," Owen said to Rachel.

She didn't tip her head up to look at him. Stayed sitting in her bedroll. "I'll get up when I'm ready."

It was a small defiance. And one he wouldn't argue against. Not right this moment.

He'd go wash up quick. If she wasn't ready to go when he came back, he'd lift her into the saddle himself if he needed to.

He was standing in the creek, bare-chested and shivering, as he scrubbed his body and arms with his hands when he caught a soft gasp and a flash of movement from nearby.

Rachel stood on the bank a couple of yards away, her eyes locked on his chest in the silvery morning light. He looked down. The bruise showed stark, like a starburst spreading from the point where the other man's fist had connected. It looked worse than the one on his face.

Rachel turned away before he could tell her that he was all right. She stalked back toward camp.

Had he seen a hint of compassion in her expression before she'd turned away?

Or maybe he'd been imagining it.

I wish we'd never met.

How come she couldn't see that he was doing his best? Leo, August, even Collin needed him back at Hollis's camp.

He'd made a bad choice in a fit of weakness when he'd told her about the eastbound caravan. If they'd carried on with Hollis, he'd have already been in a position to help. Now he was marooned out here. Surely they would catch up at the pace they traveled, often long into the night, longer than

Hollis would drive his troupe. But Owen still felt the worry and urgency. It wasn't enough.

He wasn't enough.

Donahoe's crony had gotten the drop on him.

And Rachel didn't want him.

She was standing near her horse when he returned from the creek. Molly was strapped to her chest but there was something off about Rachel. The stoop of her shoulders, maybe.

Doc was kicking dirt over the last embers of the fire. He came to Owen before he got into the saddle.

"I'm concerned about your wife," he said in a low voice.

His wife.

They'd made a convenient arrangement, but now he wished for it to be true. For him to be able to turn back time, figure out a better way...

Maybe even a way to win her over.

"She needs rest," he continued. "She was up more times last night than she has been before."

Owen knew. He'd heard, aware of her even as he slept.

"It hasn't been that long since she gave birth," the doc said. "Her body is working to feed the baby. All the long days in the saddle are wearing, even for you and for me."

Owen shook his head. They had to keep going. He had to help Leo and August and Collin.

Doc sent a concerned glance back at Rachel before going to her. They stood near the horses, Rachel holding up Molly's chin while Doc peered at the baby's neck.

Was there a chance she'd ever forgive him?

When her gaze met Owen's, her eyes flashed. Her cheeks were flushed. Angry?

"Time to go," he told the Doc.

No, Rachel would never forgive him.

But if the man hunting Stella reached the wagon train first, he'd never forgive himself.

* * *

Was that a cloud covering the sun?

Rachel shivered and squinted against the mid-afternoon light. There had been wide, flat clouds since mid-morning, scuttling across the vivid blue sky. Maybe the cloud momentarily blocking the sunlight was the reason for the peculiar chill sensation that crept over her.

Had there been that many clouds?

And had the colors in this stretch of rocky prairie been quite so vivid just yesterday?

No. The chills that had wracked her body during the night couldn't have been from the cloudy sky. She'd probably put her bedroll too far from the fire. She'd wanted as much distance from Owen as possible.

Maybe last night's chills were entirely her fault.

When would this day of riding end?

She was so tired of riding. Her legs and back had gone stiff and sore. Not to mention the areas that were still sensitive from giving birth.

She'd shifted something in the blankets Owen had crafted for her saddle. There was a lump where none had been before, and it had annoyed her since yesterday. But she wouldn't ask the infuriating man to fix it. She wouldn't tell him anything at all.

She squinted at the far horizon. Was that a tall tree? Or perhaps a cloud floating up into the sky?

She definitely wouldn't tell him about the growing ache

low in her belly. It had started before dawn, about the time of Molly's last feeding.

Molly!

Rachel's swirling thoughts were as nebulous as the clouds dancing across the sky above. For a moment, she'd forgotten about Molly. But Molly was here. Safe and sound, tucked against her and wrapped snugly.

Molly's face was scrunched in her sleep, her tiny nose bunched and brows drawn. What was she dreaming of as that little bow of a mouth pursed and relaxed?

Rachel dreamed about Owen. Or at least she had this morning, before she'd been rudely awakened by him talking with Doc, getting ready to nudge her shoulder.

She'd dreamed about the way he'd held her when she'd been in those last frantic throes of labor. He'd been a plank of strength behind her, supporting her weight, his arms strong and steady around her. When she'd woken alone in her bedroll, she'd had such a moment of disorientation that she'd almost burst into tears.

She'd loved Evan, but he hadn't made her feel as safe as Owen had in those dreamlike moments.

That Owen had disappeared completely.

She found herself frowning at the man's back as he rode several dozen yards ahead of her, the pack horses tethered behind him.

Today's Owen was single-minded in his determination to get back to Hollis's caravan. Gone was the man who'd walked and held Molly, singing softly to her. Who Rachel had *thought* she could trust.

She hated him.

Except...

If she hated him, why would she dream of him holding her?

She could barely hold onto her thoughts. Her anger had flushed away the shivery feeling and now she felt overwarm.

She wanted off this horse. Riding for hours and hours every day was mindless and boring.

Tears pricked her eyes.

She wanted to lie down.

In a real bed. A bed with a feather-tick mattress and a blanket, cool and clean from the line.

Why must she fight so hard and never receive what she wanted?

She could demand, cry, beg, scream to the four corners of the earth... and she was still powerless.

Still dependent on Owen for her very survival.

That's why she hated him. He'd taken from her what little agency she had when he'd confronted Donahoe. He knew she couldn't survive without him out here. She wouldn't last more than a day or two.

She wanted to cry.

Maybe a tear even fell.

Another chill fell over her, and she raised the hand that wasn't holding the reins to rub her arm.

Doc had been riding behind her, but all of a sudden his horse was only a few feet from her side.

"Are you feeling all right? You haven't said much today."

She opened her mouth to tell him that she wanted to be left alone. Doc was in cahoots with Owen. They spent too much time sitting around the fire talking at night for her to trust the man. But she found herself blurting, "I'm cold."

Doc's brows drew together. "You're cold?"

His gaze fixed on her face, and he frowned. He didn't usually frown like that.

The pain in her stomach began to pulse in time with her heartbeat. She moaned a little—she didn't mean to—and leaned forward, clutching the saddle horn.

She had to think of Molly. Stay on the horse.

"Owen!" Doc's bark of a shout startled her, and she realized she'd closed her eyes. Why had she done that?

"Let's stop for a minute." Doc's command was gentle but firm.

I don't want to stop. She tried to get the words out, but suddenly her mouth wouldn't move.

Doc was off his horse, standing beside her. When had they halted?

"She's burning up with fever." Doc threw the words over his shoulder.

And then Owen was there beside her.

She felt a beat of deep relief and, at the same time, deep anger.

"Let's get you down from there." Owen couldn't seem to stop bossing her. She heard it in his voice, though his face seemed to be going blurry.

"Don't touch me." She meant to say the words loudly, but they emerged only in a whisper.

"I'm real sorry, sweetheart, but we need to get you down."

His hands at her waist exerted a gentle pressure, but it was enough to make her cry out. Stars danced across her vision.

"I'm sorry, sweetheart. I'm sorry." She heard Owen's murmur as he hauled her off the horse. If he was so sorry, why didn't he stop? Why did the man never *listen* to her?

She couldn't see the sky even as she felt them lie her flat on her back.

"Molly," she whispered.

Owen's hands were gentle as he unwrapped Molly, who protested with a tiny cry that brought tears to Rachel's eyes. Doc's hands were firm as he probed her stomach. Nothing hurt until he reached her lower abdomen and then she couldn't suppress a cry. Tears streamed from the corners of her eyes as pain radiated outward from where the doctor was pushing on her.

"You're hurting her," Owen said, sounding furious. And close. Was he still holding Molly?

"Her fever and this swelling in her abdomen worries me. Infection may have set in."

"Infection?" Owen's voice seemed to fade in and out.

"Inside her. From the birth."

She couldn't understand what they were talking about. But the cold chills were gone, and now she was burning up again.

"I'll get her some water. We have to help her."

"If we can't get her fever down, we might lose her." But Doc's voice was fading out now, too.

Or maybe it was her.

Everything went dark.

Eighteen

"WHEN CAN RACHEL HAVE MORE MEDICINE?" Owen demanded.

It was late afternoon. Doc sat near a small fire that Owen had built earlier. When the older man glanced up at Owen, his expression was haggard and every muscle inside Owen seized up with anxiousness.

"Not for hours yet." There was a resignation in Doc's tone that Owen hated.

He wanted to shake the man.

He wanted to punch something.

He wanted Rachel to punch him.

"It might help if you bathed her face again. We've got to get that fever down."

Fine. Owen needed something to do with his hands.

He grabbed a pail and stalked to the small creek burbling nearby. Doc hadn't moved when he returned.

Owen faced the crude lean-to he'd constructed in a manner of hours last night. Rachel had been so still, so vulnerable, never regaining consciousness after they'd taken her off the horse.

He'd needed more than a tent as her protection from the outdoors. It was only two small trees he'd chopped down and into pieces which provided some protection when rigged together as two walls that formed an angled back to the shelter. The tent he'd cut apart to make a roof and a flap to cover the front.

She'd be furious with him for destroying her tent.

He paused for a moment outside the structure, sent a prayer winging heavenward. *Please God, let her wake up and be furious at me.*

He lifted the flap and ducked inside, careful of Molly, sleeping in the most protected area, the back corner of the lean-to. He'd done his best to swaddle her the way he'd seen Rachel do. What would happen to Molly if Rachel never woke up?

On his knees next to Rachel, he smoothed the wispy curls away from her temple. Hanging from the lean-to wall was the small cloth he'd used the last time he'd done this, only an hour ago. He dipped the cloth in the water and gently dabbed her temple.

She didn't move. Her eyes remained closed, and she was dangerously still beneath the blanket Doc had tucked over her. Her cheeks were flushed and hot when Owen's fingers brushed against her skin.

Doc had examined her yesterday, right out in the open, while Owen had held Molly and jiggled her to keep her from crying.

An infection, Doc had pronounced. Somehow, after giving birth, her body had contracted an infection.

The words had battered Owen as he'd watched helplessly.

"Wake up," he whispered now. "Rachel, I need you to wake up."

Molly stirred, her little face scrunching up in her sleep.

Rachel only breathed shallow breaths.

Owen felt his emotions rising as he dipped the cloth in the cool water again and dabbed Rachel's neck and jaw, like Doc had shown him.

Doc had explained that her fever was fighting against the infection inside her body, but if the fever got too high, Rachel could die.

"This is my fault," he whispered.

He dropped the cloth in the bucket. The weight of his emotions growing too much to bear. He dropped his head in his hands. She'd needed rest after Molly's birth, and he'd foolishly forged ahead. First to join the eastbound wagon train. And then in his hurry to get back to Leo and August.

This was his fault.

What if he'd found a way to protect them better, stayed put for a couple of days after the birth? He could've crafted a lean-to like this, something to make them safer.

What if they'd never left Hollis's wagon train to begin with? Maddie could've assisted with the birth. Rachel could've ridden in a wagon these days when she needed rest.

What if he'd told her how much she'd come to matter to him? Would it have changed her mind about leaving the wagon train?

He felt the terrible weakness pressing on him as his emotions deepened. He almost kicked the water bucket over in his haste to get out of the now suffocating lean-to.

Doc glanced up when Owen rushed outside, but he felt as if the weakness was about to spill out of him so he stalked past the other man.

Past the fire.

Splashed through the creek, uncaring that his socks got wet inside his boots.

He stopped well away from their little camp, stood with his fists pressed into his eyes. Unable to stop the weakness from overcoming him.

He'd tried so hard to be strong. But he wasn't.

Tears fell, squeezing out past his fisted fingers, sliding down his cheeks and into his beard. A sob broke free.

Rachel might die, and it was all his fault.

He'd been too distracted, too weak to make the right choices.

A throat clearing nearby told him he wasn't alone.

"Go away," he barked, as shame poured over him, burning down his body like hot oil. But he sensed that Doc was still there.

Owen scraped his hands down his face, trying to remove all traces of his weakness.

Doc stood there, ten feet away, watching.

In the distance, a tiny cry came from the lean-to. Molly.

"Go get the baby," Owen blasted.

But Doc just watched him, compassion in his expression.

Owen turned his back. He should be the one going to Molly, caring for her while Rachel couldn't. He'd married Rachel. That made them family, even if she wasn't his by blood.

But he couldn't.

"I don't want you to see—" Owen broke off. The man reacted with such compassion yesterday when Rachel had needed it. Why was he ignoring Owen's wishes now?

"I can see how much you love her," Doc said.

The words pummeled into Owen with the force of one of

those stampeding buffalo. He hadn't admitted it to himself. Had been afraid to, maybe.

"I shouldn't," Owen muttered. Rachel didn't feel the same about him. She couldn't have made it more obvious.

"It's not weakness to love someone," Doc pushed.

And the dam inside Owen burst. He whirled and took two angry steps toward the doctor. "I am weak, that's why she's in this condition. I did this to her."

It all burst out of him in a flood. If he'd chosen differently, Rachel would be healthy. If he'd been stronger, Pa wouldn't have died in that room alone, by his own hand.

He hadn't realized he was crying again until Doc placed a hand on his shoulder. Then Owen realized his eyes were swimming with tears.

"Your father made a selfish choice in his last days. I've seen patients in the last throes of illness, I've seen their terrible pain. But I don't think he meant for you to carry his choice on your shoulders."

"I should've been there." Defeat weighed heavily on him.

"Would you have stayed every second? What if you went into the other room to get him some broth to eat? Went out to use the outhouse? If he had already given up, maybe nothing could've stopped him."

Owen had never thought like that. He'd seen only how his own choices had impacted the events around Pa's death. As he considered Doc's words, turning them this way and that, a weight lifted. Freedom from the terrible guilt whispered to him.

But Rachel—

Doc must've somehow read where his thoughts had gone. "Rachel could've contracted this infection riding in a wagon," Doc said quietly.

That thought didn't help.

Molly's cries had grown into loud wails, small in the open air.

"Rachel needs you. And that baby needs you."

He worked to steady himself. Was there truth in what Doc said? It settled over Owen like a breath of peaceful breeze. Pa had made his choice. It wasn't weakness to care, to grieve what had happened. Maybe even this infection wasn't Owen's fault.

But if he lost Rachel...

"If she's got any chance to fight off this infection, she'll need her strength. We need some game to make broth. And it wouldn't hurt for you to tell her how you feel."

"Can she hear me?"

She hadn't roused once.

Doc shrugged. "She can probably feel your presence."

Owen turned to thank Doc for setting him straight, for everything, only to find Doc's wistful gaze on the horizon.

"I... lost my wife. And—" Doc shook his head. "Every day, I wish I'd had one more chance to say I loved her."

Owen strode back toward the lean-to. Molly needed him. Rachel did, too. And he found himself wishing right along with Doc.

He wished for a chance to tell Rachel he loved her.

* * *

Rachel's eyes fluttered open. She felt as if she was waking from a very long dream. She had the sense that time had passed, but how long?

It took a moment for her eyes to focus in the unfamiliar surroundings. Where was she?

She seemed to be lying inside a crude structure of sticks and tree limbs. And... canvas?

She reached up with a sluggish hand to touch her hair, only to find it matted to her head, sticky with old, sickly sweat. Yuck.

The canvas door of her little triangle house was open, and she could see out to where a small fire crackled and glowed. There were woods beyond, but she couldn't see past that. Someone had strung a clothesline and... was that her dress, flapping in the breeze?

The sun was going down, the sky a deep blue that meant it was time to settle in for the evening. Someone had been cooking over the fire recently. She could smell the scents of roasting meat and coffee.

Her stomach panged in hunger. Behind the hunger came a deeper pulse of pain, low in her abdomen. This was a pain she remembered, one that had radiated throughout her entire body. But it was less now. Dulled.

There was something she was forgetting...

Molly! Where was Molly?

Frantic, she twisted her head. She saw a little nest of blankets in the back corner of her hut. But no Molly.

Just that small movement made her realize how weak she felt.

But that didn't matter. She needed to find Molly.

She pushed up on one elbow, the movement causing the ache in her belly to flare into flames. She couldn't help the low moan that escaped her lips.

Movement came from outside her shelter, as if someone had stood up from a spot she couldn't see. She didn't know who was out there, didn't know whether it was Doc or Owen, but surely they'd know where Molly was.

A leg appeared in the edge of the opening, then Doc ducked inside. The shelter wasn't tall enough for him to stand, so he knelt beside her. He hadn't shaved, and his expression was haggard, his eyes dull.

"Where's—" Her voice was hoarse from disuse. She coughed, the motion tearing fire through her belly. "Where's Molly?"

His eyes brightened at her words. Doc placed a gentle hand on her shoulder, probably because she was ready to get up and find her daughter.

"She's fine. Owen has her. You need to lie still. You're very sick."

Owen had Molly.

Relief stormed through her as she sank back down to the pallet.

Doc lifted a dipper of water to her lips. It tasted sweet, and she guzzled as much as she could until he took the dipper away.

She had a flash of memory. Someone spooning water between her parched lips.

"What's wrong with me?" she whispered.

"Infection. I've seen it before, after a baby is born. Some women don't survive." If she wasn't mistaken, there were tears in his eyes.

"I am sorry to be such a burden," Rachel said. "How many days have I been out?"

"We've been camped here for three days."

Three days. "Is Molly, all right?" Her voice shook with the force of her worry for her daughter.

"We've done the best we could for her. You roused a few times and were able to feed her."

Rachel remembered those moments as if in a fever dream.

"Owen distilled some very diluted broth and was able to get her to suck on a cloth and take some of it."

Owen. She remembered his urgency and fear about reaching the wagon train. He must be furious with the delay. Furious with her. Maybe it was a godsend that he wasn't here this first time that she came awake.

"Owen must be angry."

Doc shook his head, his expression serious. "I think you'll find otherwise."

What could he mean? Owen had been so intent on reaching Hollis's wagon train, protecting his family. He'd be angry at the delay.

"He's the one who has been caring for you day and night. I've had to argue with him to get him to take rest so that he wouldn't make himself ill."

That. That sounded like the stubborn Owen she knew. But why would he do that?

More memories flitted through her mind. Owen, holding her when the worst of the fever ravaged her, similar to how he had held her when she had been in labor. Or had she dreamed that too?

Owen brushing a tender kiss at her temple, his whispered words begging her to wake up, to come back to him.

What was real and what was imaginations caused by the fever?

Doc left the shelter for a moment and came back with a bowl of savory smelling broth. "You need to eat if you can stand it. You've lost a lot of strength fighting off the fever."

He helped her prop herself up a little, tucking a folded blanket beneath her. He tipped several spoonfuls of broth into her mouth when she was too weak to do it herself. And then she couldn't stand any more.

He was putting away the bowl when he said absently, "Owen is devoted to you. He loves you very much."

"No, he doesn't." The automatic denial sprang to her lips.

Doc grinned a little. "And I think you return his feelings."

Now she frowned. She thought about Owen cuddling Molly, singing to her, thought about the things he'd done to take care of Rachel after the birth. How protective he'd been in Donahoe's camp. But she couldn't love Owen.

Tears sprang to her eyes. "I told myself after I lost my first husband that I wouldn't love again."

But she had fallen. For Owen. Even though she hadn't meant to.

"We don't always have the choice. I fell in love with my wife the first time I saw her."

He had never mentioned a wife before, and she noticed the desperate grief in the lines of his face.

"I don't want to be powerless," she said.

She'd suffered through her father's decisions, which she had no choice but to obey. Evan had brought her on this journey West when she'd been frightened to come. And Owen had made a careless decision when he'd confronted Donahoe.

"Loving someone does give them some power over you," Doc said in a considering way. "But it goes both ways."

She thought of the way that Owen had given her the choice whether or not to go and find the eastbound wagon train. He'd given her the choice to marry him.

He'd panicked when he had heard about the man who might be hunting Stella. Maybe he had reverted to bossy and controlling behaviors, but she could understand why when he was worried about his family.

Owen was a good man. But she still didn't know whether she could trust him with her heart.

"God has held you in His hands these past days," Doc said. "The real question is whether you can trust in God and His will for your life." He paused. "Maybe God put Owen in your path for a reason."

God had brought her through this terrible sickness, even if she had a long recovery in front of her. He'd brought Doc to them when she'd had a desperate need.

Before that, God had given Rachel an escape when the wagon train had been attacked. He had given her Evan, a husband who loved her. Glinda and Simon.

God had always been watching over her. Even if she didn't like all the circumstances that had happened. Even if they had terrified her. God had brought her to this moment.

Peace washed over her as the realization settled deep in her heart.

Maybe there would be future times where she felt powerless. She didn't know what God had in store for her and Owen. They'd agreed to marry each other as a solution to help her get back home. Was it possible that God had a different plan this entire time? That He might give her the desire of her heart? A desire she hadn't even realized until now?

Nineteen

RACHEL MUST HAVE DRIFTED off again because she came awake to a baby's plaintive cry.

Molly.

It was dark outside the shelter. Someone had closed the flap so she could only see a sliver of night sky through it, but an orange glow from the fire lit the night. This time, when she pushed up on her elbow, she felt stronger. The pain in her belly was still there, but less.

She heard a man's soft murmur.

Owen. He sounded as if he was just outside.

"I'm awake," she said.

The canvas flap pulled back, and the fire's glow revealed Owen holding Molly against his shoulder. One big hand held her weight while the other supported her head.

Owen's gaze searched Rachel's face. She didn't know what he was looking for, but the stark relief in his expression hit a tender part inside her. He made no effort to hide the shine of moisture in his eyes. Was that what was different about him?

"There you are," he said softly.

Molly wailed, and he reluctantly broke their stare to take the baby from his shoulder and glance down at her. "There's your ma," he said in an even softer voice. "Ain't we happy to see her?"

They were?

He stooped, placing Molly's warm, wiggly body against Rachel's chest. She almost melted with the relief of holding her daughter again.

She'd believed Doc when he'd said Molly was safe with Owen, but it was a different thing to hold her daughter close again. Owen must have seen the emotion in her expression, because she caught the faint smile as he ducked his head and backed away.

Molly nuzzled her face into Rachel, clearly ravenous. And Rachel's body responded in the way God had meant it to.

She was unbuttoning the front of her dress when she registered Owen leaving. "Stay."

He was already out of the shelter by the time she got her rusty voice to utter the word. She could see his legs and torso, not his head or shoulders.

Even so, she watched him hesitate. They'd had such a terrible fight, thrown awful words at each other. Would he walk away now?

Molly made a tiny noise as she began to suckle. Rachel pulled one corner of her blanket over the baby's head for modesty as Owen ducked through the mouth of the shelter again. If anything, his gaze was even more searching. She didn't know how to answer the questions in his eyes—not yet. But when she couldn't hold his gaze, she patted the ground next to her.

Owen sat, his long legs extending out of the shelter.

"You'll want something to eat. Won't you?" He sounded a

little rusty, too. A little tentative. Not like the confident Owen she'd grown to appreciate.

"In a bit." What she really wanted was to wash. The scent of sickly sweat clung to her, a holdover of the fever she'd fought.

Awkwardness descended between them, all of the feelings she'd only just acknowledged to herself bubbling beneath the surface of her skin.

"I'm sorry that we had to stop and camp here," she blurted.

Owen's eyes cut to her. His fingers plucked at the fabric of his trouser leg, as if he felt this nervous energy coursing between them, too. "It's been a rough few days."

She nodded. She'd expected him to be angry about the delay, hadn't she?

She breathed in deeply, ready to apologize again. "I know you're worried for your family—"

He bumped her thigh gently with his elbow. "I meant I've been out of my mind with worry that I was going to lose you."

His earnest words sent a single tear spilling down her cheek. Owen watched its path, though he didn't reach for her.

"I—" She didn't quite know what she'd meant to say, but a jaunty whistle approaching interrupted, all of a sudden reminding Rachel they weren't alone.

Doc.

Molly's eyelids were drooping, and her mouth fell away in a sleepy, satisfied smile.

Rachel quickly buttoned her dress as Doc's whistle cut off.

"Is our patient awake?" He sounded overjoyed at the

prospect just before he appeared in the doorway. "Have you had some water?" he asked.

She moved to sit up, still holding Molly. Grateful when Owen's arm came behind her back to support her. The strength in his arm and shoulder was a reminder of how he'd held her—it hadn't been a fevered dream, had it? His tender care for her had been real.

"What I'd really like is to move about a bit. And a bath."

Doc's expression spoke concern, and he exchanged a look with Owen.

"Owen can help me," she said.

Her husband's gaze landed on her. He nodded without looking away. "I won't let her overdo it."

She might've wrinkled her nose at that, but she wanted to wash up more than she wanted to argue.

Doc took little Molly, who was already drifting off to sleep. Owen carefully backed out of the shelter, reaching out both hands for Rachel as she gingerly rose to her feet. She felt as wobbly as a new colt, but his steady clasp gave her something to hold onto until the feeling passed.

They left Doc and his knowing smile sitting at the campfire. Owen led her slowly to a little creek nearby.

When her ankle turned, his arm came around her waist.

"I know you must be worried about August and the others," she said, keeping her gaze ahead to where she'd take her next step. "Surely we can go on in the morning, now that I feel better."

Each day they delayed would put them that much farther behind Hollis's caravan.

"You were right from the beginning," he said. "That man who's looking for Stella had a head start—"

You were right, he'd said. Would wonders never cease?

But she argued anyway. "I feel better now. We can leave—"

His grip on her elbow grew infinitesimally tighter. "We'll leave when Doc says it's safe."

Once, that bossy tone would've irritated her into a state of irritation. But right now, she felt only warmth. And love.

He did care about her. But could that emotion someday grow into love?

"I should've told you when I started feeling unwell," she blurted.

"You had reasons not to trust me," he returned. "Valid reasons."

The man seemed determined to argue with everything she said.

She stopped walking, though they were only feet from the creek now. Turned toward him, met his intent gaze. Her fisted hands came to rest on her hips, though there was none of her usual fury in the gesture. "Would you kindly let me finish my apology—"

But he didn't.

He bent his head and kissed her.

She tasted his relief and need as his hands clasped her waist, dislodging her fists. He wanted her even closer. They were finally in agreement, so she put her arms around his neck, her fingers delving into the soft hair at his nape.

His hair was shorter. She pulled back slightly, breaking their kiss.

They were both breathing hard, his eyes glittering down at her. A small smile curved his lips.

"You cut your hair," she said. That was what was different about him. "And trimmed your beard."

He had the grace to look slightly sheepish. "I figured I better give myself every advantage if I am going to win you."

Her heart leaped. He'd figured *that*?

"You look very fine," she whispered. Her fingers played with the soft hair.

The compliment and their closeness made the intimacy between them feel like a soap bubble on the verge of popping.

"Meanwhile I am in desperate need of a bath—"

One of his hands left her waist to cup her jaw. "You're the most beautiful thing I've ever seen."

The words brought a flush to her cheeks.

"Especially when a few days ago, I thought I might never get to look into your eyes again." His thumb brushed her jaw. "Hear you arguing with me..."

It was her turn to shut him up with a kiss. He was smiling when their lips touched—maybe she was too.

His kiss was tender and gentle. There'd be time for passion later, when she gained more strength. For now, she reveled in the knowledge that she loved him, and that he must care for her too.

There were still words that needed to be said. Nothing had been settled about their marriage, about their future.

But for these moments, she was content to be held. Content to be his.

* * *

Owen didn't want to stop kissing Rachel, but he sensed her energy flagging as she leaned more heavily against him.

He broke from her lips but couldn't quite set her away from him yet, so he brushed a kiss against her cheek and then her temple, and finally, the crown of her head.

He couldn't believe he was holding her like this. That she was in his arms without protest.

"You'd better wash up," he said into her hair. "If you've still got a mind to. I could hold you like this all night, but I know Molly'll fight me to have you all to herself."

She swayed backwards just a bit. His stomach pitched at the stars reflecting in her eyes. He set her back before he gave in to the urge to hold her close again.

"Is she really all right?" she asked.

He nodded. "She spent a couple of unhappy nights a little hungry, but Doc helped out. He doesn't think she was suffering."

Relief flooded her features. He felt an echo of the same in his very bones. He loved Molly like she was his own child. He wanted the three of them to be a real family.

He hadn't broached the subject with Rachel yet, quite aware Rachel had her own needs.

He helped her sit on the creek bank with her feet in the water. Stepped back as she splashed her face.

"Want me to fetch you a clean dress?" he asked.

The light in her eyes was answer enough. He left her there on the bank and jogged back to the camp to grab her clothes, along with a towel and blanket and the soap she'd surely want.

He hurried back, aware that she might be nervous in the dark.

But the night was quiet around them. He and Doc had been vigilant, and while there'd been a deer track downstream this morning, there was no sign of any predator—animal or human.

Rachel gave him a grateful smile when he returned with the items he'd brought. He moved off a few yards, far enough that when he turned his back she had privacy but close by if she needed him. He could reach her in a matter of moments.

I'm not sure I will ever love anyone the way I loved Evan.

He'd asked her once to consider a different future than the one they'd agreed on. To stay with him. And the words she'd spoken to him came back now to haunt his memory.

She'd called their first kiss a mistake. Told him she didn't want to change their agreement. But the way she'd kissed him tonight sure felt different.

Old insecurities rose. What if she didn't want him after all? There was only one way to know.

"Owen?" Her voice came on a quiet murmur, carried by the breeze.

He whirled on his heel and strode back to her, noticing how her shoulders drooped. Her energy must be sapped.

"I'm finished," she said. It was in her voice, too. Exhaustion.

He thought of the terror of the past few days, worrying that she might never wake.

"Help me up?" She held one hand out to him.

Instead, he scooped her into his arms.

She squeaked a little, but her arms came around his neck. It was much more natural than the previous time he'd carried her. Or maybe she was just overtired.

"I can walk," she insisted, but a yawn overtook her words.

"I'd prefer it if you didn't wear yourself out," he murmured into her hair. He'd come back for her dress and the blanket and towel later. Or maybe send Doc.

"So we can be ready to travel," she said.

"So you can heal."

She hummed a little, low in her throat.

Doc turned his smile into his shoulder when Owen carried Rachel through their camp. The baby was awake on his shoulder and making a muffled grunting sound.

Rachel's eyes were alert when he laid her gently on the pallet in her shelter.

"Bring me Molly?" she asked.

He did, and when he was ready to back out of the shelter and give her space, Rachel grabbed his wrist.

"Stay with me," she whispered.

It took some shuffling. He stiffened when she gasped softly and pressed a hand to her stomach.

"I'm all right. Just tweaked something." She breathed more easily. "It's passed already."

And then he was lying on his side, his head on his elbow. Rachel rested against him, and Molly snuggled into her mama's shoulder, lying on the pallet.

Rachel must've been just what Molly wanted, because the little one was already slipping back into sleep.

Owen watched Rachel trace Molly's tiny features with one fingertip, his heart overflowing.

"How can God create such a tiny miracle?" Rachel whispered.

When she turned her head to look at him, he shook his head slightly. "I don't know. I only know He did."

Owen gathered all his courage in hand and wrapped his arm around Rachel's waist. When his hand closed over hers, she threaded their fingers together.

Be my wife. My real wife. But the words he desperately wanted to say stuck in his throat.

She tipped her head back to rest against his shoulder, and he followed her gaze to the starry night sky, visible through the open flap of the lean-to.

"Doc set me straight about some things," he murmured. "About how the responsibility I carry isn't mine alone."

She squeezed his hand gently.

He watched the fall of her lashes against her cheek and kept talking. "I've tried to be strong on my own for all these years... but it's really the Lord's strength that I need."

He'd been thinking on Doc's words as he'd sat with Rachel through the dark of night. He'd come to terms with past circumstances in a way that felt like freedom from the old guilt.

"Doc set me straight, too," Rachel said quietly. "Convicted me about how I should rely on the Lord when I feel powerless."

He dipped his head to press his jaw to her temple. "I'm sorry for making you feel that way." He'd made a lion's share of mistakes and deeply regretted them now. "Can you forgive me?"

"Only if you forgive me for the awful things I said to you. I only said them out of fear."

"That's easy enough."

Something hot burned behind his nose. It surely couldn't be this easy to right all the wrongs he'd done with Rachel, could it?

"I'd like to start over," he said.

She turned her head slightly at his words, as if she didn't take his meaning.

"Be a real family," he clarified. "Have a real marriage."

He felt her go very still. For a moment, he worried that he'd read things all wrong.

Or maybe he needed to take those last threads of courage and tell her everything.

"I love you," he said. "Your independent spirit, how you mother Molly in such a caring way, your resilience." He swallowed hard. "I know how much you loved Evan. I'm not asking to take his place—"

"Evan will always be in my heart," she said.

Owen's heart stuttered. A fine tension settled in his shoulders.

"But you have a place there, too."

Her words registered and the tension gathered inside him rushed out on a gusty sigh.

"I fell in love with your strength and protective nature—even though it drives me crazy sometimes. With your tenderness when you hold Molly. And when you hold me. She needs a father, and I need a husband. I need you."

Gratefulness and tenderness swamped him and he gathered her close, careful of her frailty and the baby sleeping beside her. He pressed his face into her hair as joy surged.

She loved him.

It took several moments for the truth to sink in, but then whispered promises exchanged between them. She settled against his side again, and he was conscious of her fluttered lashes as she struggled to stay awake. Yet there was one more thing to be settled.

"I know how much it means to you to go home to your mother," he said quietly. "I think we've got the supplies to make it to Fort Laramie. I've got enough money to buy more. Maybe even buy a wagon. But it'll be safer to wait and travel with another east-bound train when one travels through."

Now she scooted away from him, far enough to turn her entire body and meet him face to face. She searched his expression.

"You'd do that? For me?"

With one finger he dragged a wisp of hair off her cheek. "I spent a good part of one night listening to you barely breathing—thinking you weren't gonna wake up to give me grief ever again." His voice caught on the last words. It took a moment for him to speak again. "What I wanted most in those moments was to be with you. Wherever that is. I can work the land or get a job in some factory. I'll provide for you and Molly however I have to."

Tears filled her eyes and one slipped out, tracking silver down her cheek. He hadn't meant to make her sad.

"I think we should go West," she whispered. "Try to join up with Hollis's caravan again. You still haven't made up with your brother and sister." She smiled. "I can be happy in the West," she whispered. "So long as we're together."

Twenty

THE SOUND of a distant gunshot caught Owen's attention. He sat tall in the saddle in that nebulous time between sunset and darkness. He should've already called a halt for the day, but for the past two days, they'd seen signs of the wagon train's recent passing. New ash from campfires lit only a day ago being the most recent one. And the closer they got to meeting up with Hollis's caravan, the deeper Owen's urgency thrummed.

He looked over his shoulder to where Rachel and Doc rode a few paces behind the pack horses tethered to his saddle.

"Someone hunting?" Doc asked.

"Probably." The pioneers would conserve their ammunition when possible; Hollis had coached the hunting parties to only shoot if one had a clear shot.

Owen waited several beats, but no other shot sounded.

"I was just about to suggest we stop for the night." This Owen said to Rachel, who sat easily on her horse. Molly, who'd grown a little each day of these past two weeks, was cocooned in her nest, wrapped against her ma. Owen had taken a turn with her earlier. There was a sense of pride when he looked after his little girl. More so that Rachel trusted him with her, so that the new mother could have a short rest.

Rachel knew him; she could probably see the anticipation vibrating through his body in the saddle. A hunting party meant they were close. He was anxious to meet up with August. And with Leo and Alice.

"We should keep going," she said. "As long as you think it's safe."

She'd spoken true about trusting God for His protection out here in the wilderness. Gone was her terror of being outdoors in the dark—though she'd confessed to him last night that she was more than ready to reconnect with the wagon train.

Owen pushed his horse forward, the others following. He wouldn't go far, not when it was falling dark. It wouldn't take long for them to make camp, and the moon was fat and full, already rising over the eastern horizon. It would give enough light for them to find a safe place, start a fire, lay out their bedrolls.

He'd stop, if they didn't—

A buck with a fine rack of antlers trotted out of the copse of woods, still a good distance away. There was something off about its gait.

And then it collapsed.

Owen reached for the rifle lying across his lap. In case whoever was hunting that buck wasn't from the wagon train.

But relief and happiness soared as he recognized the distinctive horse that rode out of the woods behind the buck.

"It's August," he said over his shoulder.

Rachel's smile lit the night sky. The wagon train had to be nearby—at least within an easy riding distance. August wouldn't travel too far for hunting, not when game was plentiful.

Owen nudged his horse into a faster walk.

He was still too far away for August to hear his shout, but it would take August some time to tie the buck to his horse and drag it close enough to camp to be butchered.

Joy flowed through Owen, unfiltered and as wild as their surroundings. His brother was alive. He looked hale enough, from this distance.

Owen had left the rifle resting across his lap, at ease now that he knew who was hunting that buck. There might be more folks in the hunting party.

He was about to reunite—

His eyes scanned their surroundings out of habit. It was only by chance that he caught sight of several shadows crouched low in the tall grasses, stalking toward August, who now knelt on the ground next to the buck.

"Owen!" Rachel's urgent cry held the same terror he felt.

Wolves.

Maybe the same wolves that had attacked them.

They were closing in on August from all directions. Five, six, seven...

Seven or eight. Too many for August to fight off.

Owen reached for his rifle, pointed it into the sky before firing off a shot.

August's head came up, turning all directions, looking for who'd taken a shot.

"Wolves! August, run!" He couldn't be sure if his shout would reach his brother from here, but Rachel had already sprung into action. She'd spurred her horse into a gallop. Racing toward the danger.

Owen kicked his horse, too, and the mount leaped into a

gallop just as Rachel came even with him. Doc followed, all three of them shouting like madmen. Doc fired a shot. Owen fired another, too.

August had jumped into the saddle—he must've seen the danger.

One of the wolves lunged forward, powerful jaws snapping—but it was too far away. August turned his horse. The horse kicked out.

The wolves scattered as Owen, Rachel, and Doc rode up.

Owen was breathing hard, still gripping the stock of his rifle. His gaze clashed with August's in the growing moonlight as he reined in.

Rachel stopped her horse nearby. The animal, sensing her agitation or maybe scenting the wolves on the air, danced two steps toward Owen, who reached out a hand and grabbed the rein on this side of its head.

"You all right? Molly?"

Rachel nodded, but her mouth was pulled tight. She'd responded instinctively, riding to his brother's rescue, and he loved her for it. But she didn't want to remain out in the open with that wolf pack around.

And he didn't either.

"Need some help, little brother?" Owen slid out of the saddle, meeting August, who'd done the same, for a hearty embrace.

"What are you doing out here?" August demanded. "I thought I wouldn't see you until next year."

"It's a long story," Owen answered with a shared glance at Rachel on her horse. "Better told back in camp after we secure your prize."

He and August quickly tied off the buck, sharing the

weight between August and Doc's saddles after a quick introduction of the men.

Owen had just stepped up into his saddle again when hoofbeats pounded close.

"State your business—" That was Leo's voice, cut off when he caught sight of Owen and Rachel and the horses. Two other men from camp had come too, their horses blowing as if they'd been pushed to run.

"We heard gunshots," Leo said.

"Wolves," August said. "Almost got me. If not for Owen..."

Owen had set aside his emotions but now realized how close it had been. August might've been killed. Or perhaps escaped with a dangerous injury. God had put Owen here at just the right time to save his brother. Hot emotion settled in his chest as the realization washed over him.

There was no warm welcome from Leo, only an order to get back to camp.

Owen heard Leo muttering with the man riding beside him about no more solo hunting parties.

One of the men with Leo rode out ahead. By the time they reached camp, folks had gathered to meet them.

August let several of the other men take care of butchering the buck, and another two passed them on their way out of camp, rifles at the ready to keep watch.

Owen helped Rachel out of the saddle, and they were swept into a flurry of hugs and backslaps.

"You have a baby!" Ben cried when she spotted them.

Felicity was just behind her, her gaze landing on the spot where Owen's hand rested at Rachel's lower back. Her eyes danced.

Alice threw her arms around him. He hugged his sister, laying his cheek on top of her head.

"I've missed you, sprite," he said.

He couldn't help noticing that Alice didn't greet Rachel at all. But his wife was in conversation with Felicity, no doubt detailing some of their adventures.

There was another notable absence. While folks were gathered, chatting excitedly, Leo had disappeared. Owen spotted him at his wagon, leaning inside. Evangeline might be tucking Sara into bed.

Molly fussed, and he lost track of his brother for the moment.

"This time of evening, she only wants her pa," Rachel explained to Felicity, who was looking on in evident delight.

He took Molly in his hands, smiled into her perturbed little face. She took one deep breath and quieted.

He'd come to believe they'd bonded during those long nights when Rachel had been down with the infection, both of them needing her so desperately. He'd done his level best to comfort and care for Molly. She was most content when her ma held her, but Rachel was right. This was their special time.

He loved his new little family fiercely.

And when he looked up and saw Leo still avoiding the celebration, he felt the same kind of fierce love for his brother.

He left the excited voices behind and went to Leo.

"I'm sorry," he said before he even got near. "I was arrogant and controlling." He'd come to terms with his faults out in the wild. He might not ever be able to relax knowing how dangerous the trail they followed was, but he could admit that he'd overdone it and put a wedge between him and his family.

"And defensive," Leo said. But there was relief and some other emotion Owen couldn't name in his expression.

"And defensive," Owen echoed.

Leo raised his brows at Molly in Owen's arms. Owen gave him the most open expression he could.

"Our pa wasn't a perfect man." Owen still couldn't forgive him for ending his life the way he had. "And I can't say why he left you and Alice. Maybe that fault was his alone, because I can't imagine walking away from Rachel and this little one."

A softness entered Leo's expression.

"And I don't want to walk away from you," Owen said. "We're family. And that means something."

Leo swallowed hard. "It does. And I'm sorry, too."

Peace settled over him. Maybe there'd still be things to talk about, but for now he had his brother back.

Owen and Leo rejoined the group that was now talking about celebrating with music after supper.

From across the way, his gaze clashed with Rachel's as Leo gave details about what he'd missed while he'd been absent from the caravan.

He had everything he wanted right here.

Rachel watched Owen and Leo embrace, Molly held carefully against Owen's shoulder.

She knew how Owen had wanted this reunion—he'd admitted as much a few nights ago over the campfire, while Doc had been sleeping in his bedroll nearby. A bittersweet feeling rose inside her. Owen had been reunited with his family, and from the looks of it, had made up with Leo.

She'd never had a resolution with Daniel. When he'd died, their relationship had been fractured—maybe beyond repair.

As Owen and Leo walked back to join the group of bigger family and friends, Owen's eyes searched until they landed on her. Some fine tension leached out of him as he smiled at her.

Just as it always did, her stomach turned a slow flip.

The excitement of Owen and Rachel's homecoming spilled over through dinner. The men who'd done the butchering returned to camp, and Rachel was relieved of any cooking duties. It wasn't long before she watched Molly being passed from Owen to Leo.

Belly full, she couldn't help smiling at the two strapping men who looked so much alike. They cooed over her daughter like two lovestruck fools. Exactly how she felt about Molly every time she looked at her.

The dishes put aside for later, Collin had pulled out his fiddle and the sound of it tuning rose over the noise of conversation. It seemed the feeling of celebration was to continue into the night.

Alice brought Owen his guitar. He was standing across the fire, next to Leo, far enough that Rachel couldn't hear what was said between the two, but Owen beamed at his sister.

Coming west had been the right decision. It settled there inside her. She still didn't know what the future had in store, what other hardships they might endure during this journey, but Owen was settled and happy.

Alice glanced over her shoulder as if she felt the weight of Rachel's stare. Her eyes cut away quickly. Rachel felt a tug in her spirit. One person wasn't happy to see her. And that was Rachel's own fault.

"I think this belongs to you." Stella appeared at Rachel's elbow, distracting her. Stella held a sleeping Molly. She looked up from the baby. "Do you mind if I hold her for a bit? It's been years since I've held a baby."

Rachel didn't mind. Stella settled on a crate next to her.

The men broke into a rollicking song, and Rachel couldn't help remembering another night of song. Owen's silly bow to her over his guitar. The way he'd looked at her.

Maybe he was thinking about the same night, because he wore an enigmatic smile even as he strummed—a smile she'd seen most often just before he'd kissed her.

She couldn't get enough of his kisses.

Collin leaned over and said something. Owen laughed, a hearty laugh that she felt in her bones.

"Owen has been worried about you," she told Stella.

The other woman's expression went carefully blank. Rachel didn't know what she was hiding, but she knew how much Owen cared.

"Doc has been traveling with us, and we've grown to trust him. He's the one who told us a man passed through the other caravan looking for a woman he claimed was his niece. This man had a sketch, and it sure seemed he was describing your sister. Or you."

Stella's throat worked as if she was swallowing hard.

"Owen cares about his family," Rachel confided. She could only hope she wasn't making this worse. "He is a fierce protector—and terribly loyal. He'll put himself in harm's way to protect you—but it would be better to know what he was protecting. So he can—so we can all—be prepared."

Stella had gone pale before a look of fierce determination crossed her features.

"I'll speak to Owen—and Leo. But first I'll need to talk to my sisters."

Ben came and pulled Rachel into a fast jig. She wasn't any good at it, but she found herself laughing with the little girl.

"You can teach Molly when she gets bigger," Rachel said, breathless, after the music had ended and the two of them had moved closer to one of the wagons.

Alice was there, half-hidden around the corner of the conveyance.

"Everything all right?" Rachel asked, surprised to see her.

Alice crossed her arms and nodded, looking to the side.

Oh.

So this was it, then. Rachel drew a deep, steadying breath.

Ben's hand slipped into hers. She glanced down for a moment, grateful for the show of solidarity.

"I'm sorry for how I acted in camp before," she blurted, looking back to Alice. "I was unkind and rude."

Alice's eyes flared wide with surprise. "I never thought I'd hear you apologize," she muttered. Then she sighed. "But what happened between us wasn't only your fault. I'm sorry, too."

Rachel released a tentative smile. "Owen loves you very much, so I'd like us to try to be friends."

Alice nodded, dropping her arms. "I can try."

"Good." It wasn't an embrace like the one Owen had received from Leo, but it was something. A new start. "Because Owen will likely want to live close to family when we reach Oregon."

"Owen won't be making a decision like that without consulting his dear wife." Her husband appeared behind her. He dropped his arm over her shoulders and planted a kiss on top of her head.

Alice watched the interplay between them. Ben ran off, calling for August.

Warmth settled in Rachel. He'd meant what he'd said in those first hours together, after she'd woken from her fever. He didn't want to control her. He wanted them to have a true partnership, one where they looked after each other.

Alice scrunched her nose. "All of my brothers are romantic saps."

Owen laughed. "I came to claim my wife for a dance."

The music was still playing, different without Owen's guitar. She let him pull her into the twirling, stomping rhythm.

She'd never danced like this before. His hand warm at her waist. His eyes soft and shining at her. His smile, lighting her up from the inside out.

She still wasn't a good dancer, but she let him lead and laughed when she accidentally stepped on his boot. Soon enough, he pulled her aside, tugging her through the darkness past the wagon guarding the circle.

"Molly—" She tugged against his hand.

"Felicity is taking a turn. I won't keep you long."

Satisfied, she followed him into the darkness.

They didn't go far.

He turned toward her, his hands spanning her waist. "I couldn't wait any longer to kiss you." He leaned down and brushed his lips against hers. "I didn't think you'd care for me to do it in front of everyone."

While he might've settled for teasing kisses between teasing murmurs, she slipped her arms around his neck and stretched up on tiptoe to deepen the kiss.

He breathed a laugh through his nose and held her closer.

She might not have a roof over her head, but she had a husband who loved her deeply and told her so often. And after tonight, she was certain she'd been adopted into his big, crazy family—whether she wanted it or not.

Together, they'd finish this journey. They would build houses and establish a new life in the Willamette Valley. But Rachel knew her true home was the man holding her tenderly in his arms. Wherever Owen was, that's where her heart would be.

God had never left her side during this journey, even in those moments she'd been terrified and felt alone. He'd protected both her and Molly, given them Owen, given them a new family and a new future.

She would never forget His providence. Or His love.

* * *

The last of the wagons splashed through the river and out onto dry land. Hollis scouted from the edge on this far side of the river, looking for anything one of the travelers might've dropped. They wouldn't come back.

Had he told the wagons to circle up after they crossed?

The niggling question bothered him.

He had. Surely he had.

The water was strong here where the river curved around a bend. Upstream were canyon walls that towered over the water. Downstream was a series of rapids that formed small waterfalls and dangerous eddies around enormous boulders. There was a natural flat area here where it was mostly safe to cross. He didn't like how high the river ran, but everyone was across now.

Except just as he turned his horse to make the crossing himself, the creaking of a wagon met his ears.

He wheeled his horse. Was there another caravan coming

up behind? He'd have thought August would've warned him if another company was close.

No. It was one of his wagons.

Abigail.

What was she doing so far behind the others?

He rode to meet her.

On the wagon's bench seat, she looked rumpled and sweaty, worrying her bottom lip with her teeth.

"What are you doing so far behind?" he demanded as she drew even with him. "You're the last wagon."

The other wagons had already moved out of sight. There'd be no one to help if she needed it. But it should be all right. All the other wagons had crossed without any problems.

"One of the wheels lost two spokes. I'm afraid if I go any faster, it'll collapse completely."

He slowed to let her pass him. Sure enough, the rear wheel on his side looked more oval than circle.

"We can repair it once you're across."

She wrinkled her nose. "Can't I cross with a rope upstream? With the other women?"

"The rope's already been taken up." The headache that had settled low in his skull now pounded with a vengeance. He'd counted the wagons as they'd crossed, hadn't he?

"I can't swim," she reminded him.

"The oxen will swim for you. Just stay calm and drive straight." The oxen were nearing the water's edge. It was deep enough that they'd have to swim over the middle part of the river for a few moments, pulling the wagon behind them.

He rode into the river a few yards upstream from her, the horse's hooves splashing his legs with water.

The canvas of her wagon brushed against a low-hanging tree branch. It stuck for a moment, then sprang free.

Hollis was already focused on the path in front of them. There was one huge boulder in the water. "You'll want to drift downstream a bit—"

"There was a beehive in that tree!"

What?

His horse went into deeper water, now covering Hollis's knees and lower thighs. He stretched forward in the saddle to see Abigail swatting at something on the seat next to her. A chunk of something light colored. Beehive?

Abigail shrieked and flapped both hands. "They're stinging my arms!"

"Watch the oxen!" Had she dropped the reins?

The wagon tilted precariously as the oxen cleared the ground beneath their feet and moved into the open water. And then the wagon was floating.

Abigail seemed unaware of the danger as she danced in the seat. "It *hurts*!"

"Watch out!" But his shout went unheeded as the wagon bumped against the boulder.

Abigail was flung out of the seat and into the rushing water.

I can't swim.

Her words from moments ago galvanized him into action. He urged his horse forward, as fast as the animal could swim.

Abigail bobbed in the current, yards away. When her head came out of the water, he saw the terror in her eyes.

"Hang on!" he called out.

His horse was a good swimmer. Hollis clung to the animal's neck, reaching out with one arm—there!

Abigail flung her arms around his neck, almost knocking him loose from his hold on the horse.

"All right, you're all right," he told her.

They were nose to nose, her eyes bright and furious and frightened. He hadn't been this close to anyone since—

He jerked his attention to where it belonged. Getting them out of the river.

A glance showed him that the oxen had done their job and pulled the wagon out onto the riverbank. They'd stopped there.

He urged his horse in that direction, his arm banded around Abigail's slight waist. He could feel the rushing water attempting to suck them toward the falls.

"We're all right. We've just got to get—"

A huge log swept through the water. Hollis tried to cling to both the horse and Abigail but the force of the impact sent him reeling. He went underwater, everything darkness.

Abigail. Where was Abigail? Had she been swept under?

He somehow got his head above water and gasped for air. Without his horse and the animal's powerful muscles, Hollis was swept away by the powerful current.

In a matter of seconds, he fell over the edge of the falls.

For my Family.

Acknowledgments

Benita, I love your questions when you read early drafts of my books. Your insights make each book better, and I so appreciate your keen mind!

As always, I'm grateful to my proofreaders Lillian, Mary-Ellen, Benecia, and Shelley for helping me clean up all the little errors (there were many!).

A special thank you for my readers

To my readers, both old and new, this book is for you.

Thank you for picking up not just this book, but the ones that came before it. Whether you've been with me from the start or just joined, your support is truly appreciated.

I hope these books provide you with a sense of escape, introduce you to interesting characters, and always leave you with the heartwarming feeling of falling in love.

With sincere thanks to (listed in alphabetical order by first name):

Abigail Biehl, Adrianna, Agnes P, Aileen, Alison, Alison Cash, Alissa Burns, Allison Proctor, Amanda Zannini, Amber Kraker, Amber Russell, Amelia Colon, Amy from TN, Amy Kathleen Shippy, Anastasia Corbin, Andi P, Angela Smeilus, Angela Young, Angie Howie, Anita Filomena, Anita Kirk, Ann Badder, Ann McCorvey, Ann. Ellison, Anna Krug, Annette, Annie, April Raulerson Hinson, Araina, Austin DBrass, Ava Leah, B i r g i t, Barb Gary, Barb kaake, Barbara Jenkins, Barbara Robinson, Barbara VanNorman, Barbara Weintz, Becky Marable, Becky Pickering, Becky Williams, Bernadette Mihalicz, Bernice Kennedy, Bernie, Beth Fullerton, Beth Heydn, Beth Lewis, Beth Maddux, Betty Ann Sharpe, Betty Armstrong, Betty Jane Allman, Betty Neil, Bev Ward, Beverly Laude', BobbieMcC, Bonnie Heringer, Bre Simpson,

Brenda (Holmes), Brenda B. Whidby, Brenda K Coulter, Brenda Witt, Briana, Bridgette K. Shippy, Brittany McEuen, Bronwyn Leanne, Brooke Burger, Bud Bivens, Bunny Albright, bunnydoodles, Callie Marshall, Carla Burner, Carla Toppass, Carol A. Foose, Carol Gehringer, Carol Randle, Caroline Hattrich, Carolyn Bryant, Carolyn Phillips, Cassie, Cassie, Cassie Bowerman, Cate VanNostrand, Catherine Boomer, Catherine Danielczyk, Catherine Taylor, Cathy, Cathy B, Cathy Genna, Ceci, Celia Miller, Chasity Easterwood, Cheryl, Cheryl Davis, Cheryl Ferrier Mayo, Cheryl Lynn Entrekin, Cheryl Marrama, Cheryn Porter, Cheyanne D.Fowler, Chris Meiser, Christie Davis, Christine Brown, Christine Spaulding, Christine Walker, Cindy, Cindy Beam, Cindy Fetner, Cindy H. Jensen, Cindy Regnier, Cindy Robinson Salazar, Cindy Rosinski, Clair, ClaireBlue, Clara Frazier Johnson, Cloe Caldwell, Colin Bell, Colleen, Colleen Bilawchuk, Colleen Clements, Colleen Flynn, Colleen Laginess, Colleen Marie Lynch, Connie, Connie K. Peacock, Connie mae, CoraVee Caswell, Courtney Bruhn, Crystal, Crystal Stewart, D'Ann, Dacia, Danita, Darla Donnenwirth, Darla Stapleton, Darlene, Darlene Ruth Paterson, Dawn, Dawn Ard, Dawn Peluso, Dawne Itnyre, Debbie Frary, Debbie Gulley, Debbie Hammer, Debbie M., Debbie Meers, Debbie Pruss, Debbie Rines, Debbie Young, Debby Lucas, Deborah Blocher, Deborah Christen, Debra Jennings, Debra Rylander, Dee, DeeDee, Dellas Anderton, Denise Laramee, Diana Hardt, Dianna Garland, Dianne McQueen, dianneknecht1947, Dolores Howard, Donna Dean, Donna Duke, Donna M Porter, Donna M. Rickey, Donna R Neumann, Donna Rodgers, Dorinda Perez, Doris Combs, Dorothy Porter, Edith Isabel Bond, Elaine Kiefer, Elise, Elizabeth Jackson, Elizabeth Litton, Elly Cox, Elodie Conrad, Emily Catherine, Emily Criddle,

Emily Frazier, Emma, Esther Edge, Evelyn, Evelyn L. Regan, Fran Breece, Gabriela, Gael, Gail Ann Williams, Gail Bayne, Gail Estes Hollingsworth, Gelia, Genie, Genie Baker, Georgia, Gianna, Ginni, Glenda Stinnett, Glenda Wray Jennings, Glinda, Gloria jean, Grace K. Peterson, Hanna Geshelin, Hannah, Hannah Hoover, Heather R., HeidiLorin Callies, Holly Bleggi, Ian, Ingerlise Pietromartire, Irina, Jackie Cover Robinson, Jackie T, Jaime Fipp, Jan Garza., Jan Michelle, Jan Tomalis, Janalyn prude, Janene Petersen, Janene Woodard, Janet Benefield, Janet Fluhr, Janet Greaves, Janet La Grasta, Janet Lanning, Janice Agnew, Janice Pettry, Janine, Jasmine, Jasmine M., Jeanette Durkin, Jeanette Fallon, Jeanette Jackson, Jeanette Rothe Johnson, jeanne sheats, Jeannette Harbottle, Jeannie Ellis, Jeff Stutsman, Jeminka van Rieck, Jen, Jenn C., Jenn Neitzke, jennier, Jennifer Greer, Jennifer Huppert, Jerry G. Wilkins, Jerry Pierson, Jerrye Bell, Jessica @ A Baker's Perspective, Jessie L. Bell, Jim Jacobs, JO WITTROCK, Joan Chartier, Joan Marie, Joann Miller, Joanna B., Joannie Sico, Jodi Hoppe Wresh, Jodi Shadden, Joy Anderson, Joy Clark, Joy Kendall, Joyce, Joyce Marion, Judith Crewdson, Judith Lasseigne, Judy, Judy Belanger, Judy Faller, Judy W., Juli Silverman, Julie Carpenter, Julie Nicole Waldvogel, Julie Permenter, Julie van Heerden, Julie Young, Julie-anne, Julieanne Canny, June, Karen "Kay" Steele, Karen Gagnon, Karen Mercer, Karen P., Karen Waymire Zimmerman, Kathleen, Kathleen, Kathleen Snyder, Kathy, Kathy, Kathy Adamski, Kathy Bunbury, Kathy McQueeny, Kathy O'Shea, Kathy Redfern, Kathy Schlagel, Katie McKenzie, Katy Jones, Kay Garrett, Kelli Heneghan, Kendall Bailey, Keren Herrera, Kim J., Kriket, Kunita R. Gear, Kym Balderson, Ladette Kerr, Lana Hicks Burton, Lani Sylvan, Laura Delgado, Laura Neumann, Laurie, Laurie A S, Laurie Kirk, Lawrence

Grogan, Leann Cookson, Leann Kasper, Leland Cork, Lelia "Lucy" Reynolds, Lelia Diane or Lelia, Leslie Jayne, Leslie W, Libby King, Linda, Linda Bellar Tucker, Linda Cooper, Linda D. McFarland, Linda Duncan, Linda Farabaugh, Linda Fast, Linda Henderson, Linda Herold, Linda Marsh, Linda Myers, Linda or Miss Markham, Linda Rorex, Linda Stitt, Linda Tucker, Linda-Marie, Lisa Caddick, Lisa J Yetman, Lisa Lagnese, Lisa Parkhill, Lisa Sanetra, Lisa Schleicher, Loretta Edgar, Lori Cole, Lori Raines, Lorraine Austin, Louellen, Louise Bateman, Lournetta (Lori), Lucila Barragan, Lucy E. Zahnle, Lucy M - Billings, MT, Lynda O, Lynn Tolles, Lynne Myers, Mae Matthis Parsons, Mae S. Carr, Makayla Brokaw, Mandy Bentley, Mandy Dudley, Marg. Ullhorn, Margaret Fraleigh, Margaret N, Margarete, Margie Evan's Taylor, Margie Harris, Maria Barrick, Marianne, Marie Crider, Marina Bauman Leonard, Marlene Moore, Martha J Lindblom, Mary A Smith, Mary Ann Speel, Mary Ellen Graham, Mary Stalnaker, Mary Welch, Megan Hamsher, Melanie foreman, Melissa D., Melissa Hartwell, Melody Adina, Melody Rekow, Merry Chapman, Michele Galloway, Michelle Rhoden, Mickie Hall, Monique Cocanougher, Morgan W. Estes, Myra Limbaugh, Myrna Joy, N/A, Nana Pat Williams, Nancy, Nancy C. Vance, Nancy Lee Rapp, Nancy Scallion-Wood, Nancy T., NancyAnn, Natalie Hughes, Nataline, Natalya Lakhno, Natasha Derry, Natasha P., Nelene, Nita G, Norma, Ojone Nwosu, Pamela, Pamela Hagen, Pamela Kyzer, Pamela Sanders, Pat. Sweeney, Patrice, Patricia, Patricia B. Hawes, Patricia Bennett, Patricia Brooks, Patricia Carlo, Patricia Greene, Patricia Harris, Patsy Ezell, Patty Pauley, Paty Hinojosa, Paula H, Paulie, Peggy, Peggy, Peggy L Singer, Penny, Penny J Deakins, Priscila P., Rachelle VanAuken, Rebecca Berlo, Reid, RENATE HERRMANN,

Renée Jackson, Renee McDonald, Rhea Humphries Piziali, Rhonda, Rhonda Grant, Robin C. Justus, Rose H., Rose Milligan, Rosemarie Andreano, Ruby Thomas Gay, Ruth, Ruth Ann Campbell, Ruth Viljoen, Ruthe Threet, Sally Childs, Sally Garnaat, Samantha Day, Sandra Clinton, Sandy, Sandy Sue, Sandy T, Sara, Sara Aimee, Sara Elisabeth Downs, Sara White, Sarah DeLong, Saundra, Shannon Sharp, Sharann Lloyd, Shari, Sharon D Riggs, Sharon Gower, Sharon Link, Sharon Meier, Sharon Sands, Sharon Tudor, Sharon W. Steward, SharonAnn Piel, Shawna Moore, Shelia Williams, Shelley, Shelly Spence, Shelly Uhing, Sherry Miller Reesor, Shirley Cool Cochran, Shirley Hackman, Sonya, Stephanie Fisher, Stephanie Halcomb, Stephanie O., Sue, susan atkins, Susan B, Susan Bird, Susan Ellingwood, Susan F. Fletcher, Susan from Montana, Susan Gourdin, Susan Heim, Susan Horton, Susan Ladd, susan marie, Susan Nuss, Susan Rae, Susan Seagroves, Susan Sigler, Susie Brownback, Suzette Either, Suzette M Davis, Tami Burritt, Tami McKee, Tammy Green, Tara Peters, Tavia Curtis, Temilolu, Tena Burnes, Teresa Christianson, Teresa S, Teri P, Teri Ruth Ware, Terri Camp, Terri McNabb, Terrie Beckett, Theresa, Tina Ledbetter, Tina Rice, Tina Shannon, Toni F., Tory Updegrave, Tracy Mussman, Treasa George-Price, Trina Boston, Trinity Womack, Valorie Benson, Venessa Vintigan, Vernona Hale, Veronica, Vicki, Vicki L Boyd, Vicki Lantz, Vickie Bright, Vickiy, Vilma Akins, Viola Frere-Martin, Violet L Davis, Violetta, Virginia Butterfield, Virginia Campbell, Vivian Pearson, Wanda Banks from Southern Pines, NC, Wanda Lafferty, Wendy Olson, Wendy Ann, Willadean, Zein AlMaha Oweis (Zee)

Want to connect online? Here's where you can find me:

GET NEW RELEASE ALERTS

Follow me on Amazon
Follow me on Bookbub
Follow me on Goodreads

CONNECT ON THE WEB

www.lacywilliams.net
lacy@lacywilliams.net

SOCIAL MEDIA

Also by Lacy Williams

Christmas Bells and Wedding Vows (anthology)

WAGON TRAIN MATCHES

A Trail So Lonesome

Trail of Secrets

A Trail Untamed

Wild Heart's Haven

A Rugged Beauty

WIND RIVER HEARTS SERIES (HISTORICAL ROMANCE)

Marrying Miss Marshal

Counterfeit Cowboy

Cowboy Pride

The Homesteader's Sweetheart

Courted by a Cowboy

Roping the Wrangler

Return of the Cowboy Doctor

The Wrangler's Inconvenient Wife

A Cowboy for Christmas

Her Convenient Cowboy

Her Cowboy Deputy

Catching the Cowgirl

The Cowboy's Honor

Winning the Schoolmarm

The Wrangler's Ready-Made Family

Christmas Homecoming

Heart of Gold

SUTTER'S HOLLOW SERIES (CONTEMPORARY ROMANCE)

His Small-Town Girl

Secondhand Cowboy

The Cowgirl Next Door

COWBOY FAIRYTALES SERIES (CONTEMPORARY FAIRYTALE ROMANCE)

Once Upon a Cowboy

Cowboy Charming

The Toad Prince

The Beastly Princess

The Lost Princess

Kissing Kelsey

Courting Carrie

Stealing Sarah

Keeping Kayla

Melting Megan

The Other Princess

The Prince's Matchmaker

HOMETOWN SWEETHEARTS SERIES (CONTEMPORARY ROMANCE)

Kissed by a Cowboy

Love Letters from Cowboy

Mistletoe Cowboy

The Bull Rider

The Brother

The Prodigal

Cowgirl for Keeps

Jingle Bell Cowgirl

Heart of a Cowgirl

3 Days with a Cowboy

Prodigal Cowgirl

Soldier Under the Mistletoe

The Nanny's Christmas Wish

The Rancher's Unexpected Gift

Someone Old

Someone New

Someone Borrowed

Someone Blue (newsletter subscribers only)

Ten Dates

Next Door Santa

Always a Bridesmaid

Love Lessons

NOT IN A SERIES

Wagon Train Sweetheart (historical romance)

Printed in the USA
CPSIA information can be obtained
at www.ICGtesting.com
LVHW090056151124
796698LV00037B/727

* 9 7 8 1 9 6 0 2 4 8 1 6 9 *